SUMMER AT SAINT PIERRE

When Sally Purvis caught the night car-ferry to France, she had nothing more adventurous in mind than taking her young brother to stay with a French pen-friend in Brittany, then driving on to join her boy-friend for a holiday in the South of France. The Crate, of course, *was* rather an ancient vehicle, and her boy-friend's affections did seem to be cooling a little, but even so, to become involved in the opening of a chateau as a hotel for English-speaking visitors, by an aristocratic, if somewhat down-to-earth, French family, was the last thing she'd expected.

The result is a romantic story told against the background of rural Brittany, as a widely varied selection of holiday-makers meet up at the chateau.

Summer at Saint Pierre

by

PAT LACEY

ROBERT HALE · LONDON

© Pat Lacey 1979

First published in Great Britain 1979

ISBN 0 7091 7112 9

Robert Hale Limited
Clerkenwell House
Clerkenwell Green
London EC1R 0HT

Printed in Great Britain by Bristol Typesetting Co. Ltd,
Barton Manor, St. Philips, Bristol
and bound by Redwood Burn Ltd, Esher

ONE

The long line of cars and caravans inched slowly forward, past the immigration point and the men checking our travel documents, speeded up across a stretch of moon-washed quay and slowed again for the ramp into the giant hold of the car ferry.

" Here we go !" said Greg, my sixteen-year-old brother.

Mindful of the age of my near-vintage little car, I drove carefully up the ramp into the bowels of the ferry and was marshalled to my place behind a large and opulent Rolls. A second later, the gleaming, scarlet snout of a new sports car followed us along the track. Between the two, the Crate looked more than ever like a museum piece.

" I wonder," I mused worriedly, " If I'm doing the right thing."

Greg dragged his eyes away from the sports car and considered the Crate dispassionately. " She ought to make it to Saint Pierre," he said, " but as for the South of France, I think you'll be pushing it a bit." He smiled suddenly; the attractive, lop-sided grin that would be breaking female hearts in a year or two, I guessed. " And I meant that literally !"

As we collected our overnight luggage, locked the car

5

and walked up to the passenger deck, I wished for the hundredth time that Nigel had been able to come with me. The journey would have been free from worry in his big, comfortable saloon; first to Saint Pierre, somewhere on a rocky stretch of the Brittany coast, to leave Greg with his French pen-friend, and then down to the villa in the hills behind Grasse that several of us were sharing for the month of August.

But Nigel had been unable to get away when we'd planned and was coming later; with, I had a nasty, unsettling suspicion, Jennifer Carse, the girl he'd been friendly with before he'd met me.

It had been wounded pride, as much as the desirability of getting Greg to Saint Pierre on the day he was expected, that had persuaded me to put the Crate in for a hurried service and make the journey on my own.

At least, I reflected, the first lap of the journey was over safely. Weaving among the queues already forming for the Duty Free Shop, the Passport office and the cafeteria, I was grateful that at least we had berths booked for the night crossing.

" Coffee?" I suggested to Greg. "And then bed, don't you think?"

" Bit early isn't it? For bed, I mean."

It was now nearly midnight. I looked at my young brother more closely and realised, with a stab of envy, that he still looked fresh as a daisy or, in his case, crisp as a full-blown chrysanthemum. From the maturity of my twenty-four years, I had forgotten about the resilience of the very young. I remembered, too, that this was Greg's first trip abroad without the discipline of a school group. No matter how late the hour, the ritual of ex-

6

ploring the ship on his own would have to be observed.

I wondered briefly about Marcel Montarial, his pen-friend at Saint Pierre. Coming home to collect Greg at the end of term from the school where I taught domestic science, I'd only had the shortest of stays with my parents, and that had been spent mostly in hurried shopping expeditions; so I knew little about the boy's background.

" I'll see you in our cabin, then," I said, now. " Be quiet when you come in. It's four berth and the other two occupants may be asleep, already."

" Never fear !"

I watched him walk away, with a studied nonchalance, along the deck, then got myself into the queue for the cafeteria.

Some sort of Evergreen Club or Darby and Joan Convention was on board, I decided, noticing how many of my fellow queuers were well above the sixty mark. Festooned with cameras, string bags, travelling rugs, picnic baskets, it was amazing how they still managed to carry their trays.

I found myself sharing a table with two elderly, white-haired ladies who clearly took me to be an expert on continental travel. " What time do we arrive, dear?" asked one.

" Seven-thirty," I said, forbearing to point out that we'd just been given the information over the ship's tannoy system.

Her companion suddenly gave a tiny shriek and clapped a hand to her mouth.

" What is it, Agnes?" Her sister, as I guessed her to be, turned to me. " It can't be the gas," she confided, in a sort of whispered aside. " Our neighbour, Mr. Saxby,

7

turned it off for us. *And* the water. And he promised to go in every day and feed Winston. He's our canary. We call him Winston after dear Mr. Churchill in the war. But you wouldn't remember that, of course!"

She broke off this fascinating monologue to gaze at her sister, now scrabbling frantically in the recesses of a capacious, hessian shoulder bag. "Agnes! Not your . . . ?"

"Yes, Eve, my spectacles! I must have left them on the mantelpiece."

"Agnes, how dreadful!" It was a cry from the heart. "Well, we shall just have to go back for them, that's all."

Since we were now well out into the channel, I wondered how she proposed to manage this. At the same time, I knew I would hate to be in the captain's shoes if he had to refuse the entreaty in two pairs of big, blue eyes. I was relieved as they when Agnes suddenly let out another little shriek—this time, of relief.

"Here they are! In the middle of this magazine! Silly, little me!"

"I'm so pleased. Well, bon voyage!" I drained my cup, wished the sisters a peaceful crossing and made my way to my cabin. To find, as I had expected, that the lower berths were already occupied—by two more members of Miss Eve and Miss Agnes's party, I decided, gazing down on their sleeping faces.

There was sufficient light from the companion way outside to enable me to mount to my bunk in safety without disturbing them. Within minutes, I, too, was asleep.

It seemed like seconds, but in fact it was a whole hour

later that I was rudely awakened by Greg shaking my shoulder with a brotherly lack of respect.

"Sal! I hate to do this to you, but there are a couple of old ladies outside."

"There are three in here, too," I hissed. "Hurry up and join us!"

"Sal, you don't understand. These two have nowhere to sleep."

I recognised the concern in his voice. Raising myself on my elbow, I gave him a careful scrutiny. He wore that frozen, withdrawn expression that meant, deep down inside, he was desperately worried. The last time I'd seen it, he was cradling an exhausted puppy in his arms and demanding vengeance on whoever had abandoned it on the by-pass near our home. That puppy, now his devoted slave was probably wondering at this moment what had become of his lord and master. Old ladies without sleeping berths were probably bracketed in Greg's mind with homeless, abandoned puppies.

"You mean," I yawned, still heavy with sleep, "that we should give them our bunks?"

"Sal, I'm sorry, I hadn't realised quite how clapped out you were. Go back to sleep. Perhaps they can both get into my bunk."

The thought of two elderly ladies sharing a top bunk filled me with alarm. "They might fall out in the night. No, you're absolutely right, Greg. We can easily curl up on deck, somewhere."

It came as no surprise to discover that Greg's two old ladies were Miss Agnes and Miss Eve. "My dear, we couldn't possibly turn you out of your nice, warm bunk."

"I never sleep, anyway," I lied. "A chair will be

9

quite enough for me."

Getting them up to the top bunks took careful planning. In the middle of the operation, their friends below woke up and insisted on helping. When Greg and I eventually left, they were all sitting up in bed chattering away like starlings.

" Curling up on deck " was easier said than done. Every nook and cranny of the ferry seemed packed with holiday makers. Eventually, we shared a sheltered corner with a family from Liverpool, Mum, Dad and two very solid little girls. I know, because one of them went to sleep as completely as my arm soon did!

But somewhere between two and three in the morning, I must have fallen into a deep sleep of utter exhaustion. I knew no more until the cold, clear light of dawn filtered through my eyelids. For a moment, I lay there, conscious of an extraordinary sense of warmth and comfort.

Then I opened my eyes. Greg and the family from Liverpool must have removed themselves while I had slept. Instead of cradling my plump little girl, I was lying practically in the arms of a dark and handsome stranger and covered, apparently, by the all-enveloping folds of his travelling rug.

His head pillowed comfortably on an old, tweed jacket, he was fast asleep. Just in time, I stopped my involuntary movement away from the firm pressure of his arm. A fine way of showing my appreciation of several blessed hours of deep sleep, to jerk him awake from his own sound slumbers!

A suspicion that I was taking an unfair advantage of his unconscious state, didn't prevent me from studying intently the face only inches away from my own.

Early thirties, I decided, noticing the flecks of grey among the jet black curls. What colour eyes, I wondered, would go with dark hair and olive skin? Deep blue, perhaps, to match the pullover I could see under the rug.

A silky moustache was neatly trimmed and the hand that lay so gently on my shoulder was perfectly manicured. Definitely French, I decided, noticing the Continental cut of the shoes peeping out from the blanket and sniffing a subtle mixture of expensive cigars and discreet aftershave. And there was more than a suggestion of the Grand Seigneur in the firm mouth and well defined jaw line.

Occupation? The smooth, well kept hands spoke of a sedentary way of life but the texture of the skin was that of someone accustomed to spending long hours in the open air.

He moved suddenly, and I shut my eyes like a trap. But his arm only increased its pressure and his head nestled deeper into my shoulder. It could be the reaction of a man who has grown accustomed to a certain woman and feels instinctively for her as he begins to surface from sleep. I held my breath.

But he lay still and I dared to peep again. His lips now wore a tiny smile—as if he liked whom he was holding. Whom he *thought* he was holding!

It was time that I removed myself. Our mutual embarrassment when he awoke and discovered me in his arms was too painful to consider.

It wasn't easy to slide away from his arm without waking him, but I managed it. Within seconds, I was free and shivering in the chill morning breeze.

I stood for a moment and then bent to tuck in the

rug around the tall and, I would have thought, lean and muscular body. I hoped he wouldn't be too disappointed to find no one in his arms when he awoke. Perhaps his lady would be waiting for him when we docked. I glanced at my watch and saw that that would be happening in just over an hour.

A cup of coffee and a crisp croissant later, I was feeling fit for anything. Until that is, I collected my sponge bag from a cabin still pulsating with heavy breathing and went to wash. My early morning face was pinched and drawn, my long fair hair clinging to my head in damp tendrils and my brown eyes darker than ever with the shadows beneath.

But it was marvellous how a little, strategically applied make-up worked an instant magic. And a rose coloured head-square not only hid my hair but brought a reflected warmth to my cheeks. Soon, I was hanging over the rails with everyone else, watching the Normandy beaches come slowly nearer and feeling a sense of holiday anticipation, at last. Before long, my duty done by Greg, I would be speeding to the sunny south. And to Nigel? I hoped so.

"Ah, there you are!" Greg was at my elbow. "I've been breakfasting with our friends from Liverpool. You were so sound asleep, I left you where you were."

"Was I alone at the time?" I enquired casually.

He raised an amused eyebrow. "Well, yes! If you don't count the few hundred or so other people on board!"

I ignored this fatuous remark. "I wasn't, what you might say, leaning on anyone?"

"Not that I noticed!"

Soon, disembarkation safely accomplished, we were driving down the long, poplar shaded roads of Northern France, the Crate responding like an old, war horse to the gay tan-tivvies of the Continental models zipping past.

Although I said nothing to Greg, I recognized the driver of one of the cars; my grand seigneur, accompanied by a smart, dark-haired woman, was at the wheel of a white, sports job. Just as I thought!

Thinking of the comfort and security I had found in his arms, seemed to have a soporific affect on my brain. The long, straight road was never ending. I wound down the window, gripped the wheel and commanded Greg.

" Talk to me! Or we'll be in the ditch in a moment!"

" What about, for heaven's sake?"

"Anything! School, cricket, 'O' levels, Pop. The teen-age scene, generally."

Greg whistled. " You don't want much, do you?"

"Tell me about your friend, Gryffin. That's not his real name, surely?"

He grinned at me. "Don't you know your Alice in Wonderland? Actually, his real name is Griffiths. But ever since the day we caught him reading Alice, it's been the Gryffin. He's a great character. Spending his holidays digging his grandmother's garden and then hitching up to Scotland to help keep an eye on some rare bird or other. He's a pretty rare bird, himself!"

" Which leads me to ask after *your* holiday job. I thought you were all set to make a fortune, selling brass rubbings to the American tourists?"

" I was," Greg agreed regretfully, "until this Brittany exchange came up. Apparently, Marcel stayed

13

with Mathew Forbes at Easter on the understanding that Mathew would go to him in the summer. But Mathew's parents suddenly decided to emigrate to Canada, so the Head asked me if I'd like to take over."

" Know anything about his family?"

" Not much. His mother was killed some years back in a car crash, apparently. So he's been brought up by a great-aunt. His father travels a lot, the Head said. That's all he knew, except that he lives in this little village on the coast."

" And what time do they expect you?"

" Anytime this evening. I wrote and told them my big sister was driving me in her limousine!"

" That's asking for trouble!" But the Crate continued to purr like a contented pussy cat and the miles flowed by.

Stopping for lunch at Avranches. we even spared five minutes to gaze from the walls at the fabulous edifice of Mont St. Michel in the distance. We should easily make Saint Pierre by the late afternoon, I reckoned, which should give me plenty of time to see Greg safely settled and find myself an hotel for the night.

We drove on through sleepy hamlets of grey, granite houses, their wooden shutters peeling in the sun, their gardens gay with marigolds. In the middle of just such a hamlet, slightly larger, perhaps, because there was a shop, a petrol pump and a church, Greg suddenly noticed the red warning light on the dashboard.

" Hang on, Sal! We must be running on the battery."

I drew in between the church and the petrol pump. Greg got out and lifted the bonnet. The next moment, he was dangling a long strip of rubber between his thumb and forefinger.

14

" Fan belt's broken! Where's the spare?" He looked at me, hopefully and then with gathering dismay. " Haven't you got one? Oh, Sal, you are a ninny!"

He was right. The advisability of carrying spares on a continental car journey, had completely escaped me.

By this time, a boiler-suited figure had emerged from behind the petrol pump.

" Essence, m'sieur? Combien?"

For answer, Greg waved the broken fanbelt at him like a tired snake.

The man shrugged expressively, considered the Crate for a moment or two then shook his head ominously and wandered off into the shed beside the pump.

" Keep your fingers crossed," said Greg. " It'll be a major miracle if he's got one to fit."

Considering the size of the premises, I felt it would be a major miracle if he'd got one at all. In fact, he soon emerged with several but only, apparently, to demonstrate that none of them could possibly fit the Crate. He broke into a spate of patois that was quite incomprehensible to me.

" Breton," said Greg knowledgeably. " It's more like Welsh than French. Hardly surprising when you remember that the Celts sought refuge here from the Angles and Saxons during the 5th and 6th centuries."

" Very interesting!" I agreed. " But it's not going to get us a fan belt in a hurry!"

However, our friend was nothing if not resourceful. Arms waving, feet running briskly on the spot, it was soon made clear that a fan belt to fit could be procured from a village several kilometres down the road along which we had just come.

" Shouldn't take him long," said Greg, after we had smiled and nodded in complete agreement with whatever he was suggesting. A smart saloon was parked beside the pump but M'sieur, apparently, had other things to do. A small boy was summoned from an adjacent cottage and, with cries of urgency, despatched on a very rusty bicycle.

To our surprise, M'sieur then seemed bent on persuading us to go to church; perhaps to offer a prayer to Saint Christopher for the speedy return of our messenger—with fan belt?

I have a passion for country churches and soon we were wandering gratefully in the cool interior, heavy with the perfume from a jar of lilies beside the elaborately carved, altar screen. Surprisingly for mid-afternoon, the place was ablaze with light.

We soon discovered why. Knots of people, clad in their Sunday best, had followed us into the church, the men with flowers in their buttonholes, the women wearing the beautiful Breton coiffe, a headdress of stiffly starched, white lace.

" It's a wedding!" said Greg.

Soon the church was nearly full and our garage proprietor, his dungarees now exchanged for neat, navy serge, saw us comfortably settled in a pew well towards the front of the church. Then, obviously a man of many parts, he perched himself before a fair sized organ and began to play with great flourish and expertise.

" Here comes the bride!" Greg nudged me to my feet as a delicate rosebud of a girl, ethereal in her floating, white dress, walked up the aisle on the arm of her proud escort, a radiant procession of six, rainbow-hued bridesmaids behind. Her groom, a great strapping youth, his heart in his eyes, rose to claim his bride.

I suddenly found myself moved almost to tears by the simplicity and sincerity of the little ceremony. Would I ever find myself floating down the aisle on my father's arm towards an anxiously waiting Nigel? Somehow, I doubted it. And then, a result, perhaps, of tiredness, I found myself thinking of my grand seigneur! Awake, no doubt, he would be the most obnoxious of men, arrogant, high handed, given to bouts of undisciplined temper. Or so I told myself. But his face, I remembered, had been relaxed and gentle in sleep. He was probably a devoted family man.

While I had thought my ridiculous thoughts, the service had continued and soon, hand in hand, the couple were coming down the aisle. Along with everyone else in the congregation, I found myself nodding and smiling my good wishes.

As we all streamed out into the sunlight, several people spoke to us, but still in that musical, totally incomprehensible lilt.

We even found ourselves pressed into the photographs that were taken at great speed by a volatile young man in a bright, check suit and flowing, yellow tie. " A city gent, d'you suppose?" wondered Greg in my ear.

Then our old friend, the organist, arrived and took us under his wing, presumably explaining our predicament to the wedding party. There were murmurs of sympathy and the bride's father even went so far as to put one arm around my shoulders and the other around Greg's and lead us through the church yard and down the street in the wake of the happy couple. Before we

17

realised what was happening, he was ushering us into the village hall, a beautiful, half-timbered building, centuries old.

Inside, were long, trestle tables covered with snow-white linen cloths and every conceivable variety of food.

I glanced at Greg in consternation. " We shall never make Saint Pierre at this rate."

His answering shrug was as expressive as any I had seen that day. " I can't see our friend putting on any fan belts in the very near future," he pointed out. He was right, of course. The garage proprietor-cum-organist was still in his best suit—and obviously preparing for a good time.

It was impossible, anyway, not to respond to the good-will and friendliness of everyone around us. Soon, we were toasting the happy couple as if we'd known them all our lives.

" Well, it was worth it wasn't it?" asked Greg, some four hours later as he turned from waving to the wedding party, who had insisted upon pushing the Crate all the way down the main street.

I waved with one hand and agreed that, come what may, it had been worth it. I shouldn't lightly forget Breton hospitality. " All the same," I said, " I hope your pen friend keeps late hours!"

We travelled steadily on through the lush, wooded countryside, the Crate responding magnificently. Even so, it was quite dark when Saint Pierre began to appear on the sign posts.

" What's Marcel's exact address?" I asked.

" 'Les Quatres Vents', Saint Pierre. I think it's quite a small village."

It was. Deep in apple orchards, we had driven through it and out the other side, before we realised it.

I reversed The Crate and drove slowly back, trying to keep my anxiety under control. It was now nearly ten o'clock and I still had to find somewhere to stay after I had dropped Greg.

" I'd better ask someone," I said. But the occupants of Saint Pierre seemed to go early to bed. There was no one about in the long straggling street of tall, gabled houses, nor in the little square; but a light shone in the window of a tiny restaurant that advertised ' Les Crêpes Magnifiques '.

" After that wedding reception," I said, " I don't feel I can face another crumb, let alone a magnificent pan-cake ! "

" Oh, I don't know ! " said Greg, with the insatiable appetite of a growing youth. " It won't take a minute."

" I suppose it would be one way of finding out exactly where ' Les Quatres Vents ' is," I agreed.

So, while Greg ate his way steadily through a truly magnificent crêpe stuffed with succulent, pink ham, I chatted up the cook; a tall, dark Breton with a red kerchief around his wrist on which to mop his gleaming forehead as he bent to his task. It was no wonder we hadn't seen anyone about in the streets; the entire population of the village seemed to have gathered around the big, open fire of gleaming coals waiting for their pancakes to be cooked.

Considerable discussion ensured when I asked about ' Les Quatres Vent '. Most of it was in patois, so that I could only understand the occasional word. But the name Montarial occurred several times, usually accom-

panied by the spreading of expressive hands and the nodding or shaking of eloquent heads.

At one point, it seemed that an argument might
develop, but Monsieur le Patron would have none of it.
The altercation was quelled as quickly as it had begun.
He turned back to me and explained, slowly and politely,
and in French that I could easily understand, that ' Les
Quatres Vents ' lay about half a kilometre along the
road and was, in fact, a lodge at the gates of the local
chateau.

Greg having by now finished his crêpe, we bade the
company adieu and drove away in the direction we had
been shown. By now, I was more anxious than ever; not
only at the lateness of the hour but in case I was leaving
Greg in the centre of some hotbed of local disturbance.
Perhaps Marcel's great-aunt did a not-so-quiet line in
poaching on the chateau preserves!

By the time we reached ' Les Quatres Vents ' we were
both unusually silent. Needless to say, the creeper-covered
lodge beside the tall, wrought-iron gates, was in darkness.

We sat in the car and discussed what to do next.
There was nothing for it, we decided, but to hammer on
the door and wake up the Montarials. Clearly, there
was nowhere in Saint Pierre where we could put up for
the night. And, I suddenly reminded myself, Greg *was*
expected that evening.

Working myself up into a fair state of indignation, I
clambered out of the car and opened a wooden gate set,
so my nose told me, in the midst of a hedge of sweet
briar. Quietly, we tiptoed up a narrow garden path between grasping rose bushes; a ridiculous precaution, I
realised, in view of the reverberating clang of the heavy

brass knocker I let fall on the front door. Immediately, there came the barking of a dog somewhere behind the house. But nothing else.

"Let me try!" This time, Greg lifted the knocker and the sound was deafening.

A window shot up somewhere above our heads and a voice shouted something incomprehensible, but clearly indicative of protest. I looked up at the outline of a large male figure and found I was grasping Greg's arm in a protective fashion.

But he, apparently, considered that he was the protector. In carefully worded, schoolboy French, he explained who we were and apologised profusely for the lateness of our arrival. And did he have the pleasure of addressing the father of Marcel Montarial? He then paused expectantly.

The head at the window now being joined by another, there was a quick, sibilant exchange ending with a woman speaking in a voice that was as careful and polite as Greg's own.

'Le petit Marcel' was, apparently, up at the chateau with his Tante Jeanne. If we were to continue up the avenue of beech trees stretching away into the darkness, we would, eventually, reach the château. All would then be revealed.

At this point, the man cut into her speech with a spate of patois that seemed to include the words 'le Duc' repeated several times. But the woman obviously overrode him, and bade us a polite goodnight.

"I just hope they keep later hours at the château than at the lodge," I murmured to Greg as, having thanked our guide, we made our way back down the path. "On the other hand, I don't feel in the least like meeting anyone remotely aristocratic. I haven't had a wash since dawn!"

"Maybe Tante Jeanne is the housekeeper there," Greg suggested.

"Well, we'll soon find out."

The Crate nosed her way beneath the beeches. High above, stars shone through the dark canopy of leaves. Somewhere, an owl hooted, and was answered by another. And then we were suddenly through the trees and ahead was one of the most beautiful sights I have ever seen.

For the first time on our journey, we were near the sea. Over it, the moon rose full and golden, and at the end of its shining path, the three pepper-pot towers of the château and the rocky cliff upon which it was built, rose in jagged silhouette. I heard Greg catch his breath.

"Incredible, isn't it?" I said. "But—wouldn't you know?—except for the moon, not a light to be seen!"

"Isn't that a lamp just below the central tower?" Greg suggested.

"You could be right. We'll go and see."

And, as we descended a long incline, passed under an arched gateway let into a long, stone wall and entered a paved courtyard, I could see that a lamp was indeed burning above a massive door in the central tower. The rest of the château was in complete darkness.

"I shouldn't think," I said doubtfully, "that le Duc, if he *is* at home, will want us pounding on his front door. We'd better try the back."

"I noticed a little path going along the outside of the wall as we came in," Greg offered. "It should end up somewhere in the nether regions."

We left the Crate, lonely and forlorn in the centre of the huge courtyard. It seemed a place more accustomed to the grandeur of a coach and four than to a battered, if beloved old boneshaker.

The sea sounded very close as we crept along the shadow cast by the high wall. Approaching the right-angled corner that would bring the rear of the château into view, Greg suddenly developed an attack of the giggles. " Hope we don't meet le Duc coming the other way with a knife in his teeth!"

The idea, at that hour of the night, had me joining, almost hysterically, in his mirth.

It could have been this temporary lack of concentration on my part that prevented me from seeing what was immediately in front of my nose, or it could have been relief that when we *did* round the corner we saw, not a murderous Duke but a lighted window in a downstairs room; whatever the reason, the next moment there came a thunderous crash, as of a million tin cans rolling down a steep incline, and I was flat on my back in what must be the château's rubbish dump!

There was a second of silence as intense as the reverberating din. Then, " Sal?" came Greg's anxious whisper, " are you all right?"

My reply was lost in the slam of a door flung violently back on its hinges. Light flooded out from the château, just reaching me where I sprawled among the refuse, aware of a sharp pain in my right ankle but even more acutely conscious of the humiliating picture I must be making.

" Who's there?" A man's voice called out sharply in

French. And then he turned and shouted something into the room behind him, where I could now see the shape of a woman. The next moment, the beam from a powerful torch was shining full on to me and I heard the crunch of his footsteps as he came towards me over a stretch of gravel.

"Georges, you old devil, is that you?"

My extreme embarrassment at this ridiculous question, shocked me into using the comforting familiarity of my mother tongue. "I am looking," I said, with as much dignity as I could muster, "for Madame Montarial. I understood that she was expecting my brother, Gregory Purvis, for a stay of several weeks."

"Mon Dieu!" The exclamation of horror that escaped from the woman's lips was clearly audible. She came running down the steps, pushing the man to one side. "I thought it was tomorrow! Oh, a thousand pardons, madamoiselle!"

Quickly, I was helped to my feet and escorted up the path towards the lighted doorway. In it, there had now appeared the figure of a pyjama-clad boy, of about Greg's age.

Tante Jeanne, for she it must be, was desolated, utterly desolated, at her foolish mistake. Would I ever forgive her? Her English, I was pleased to notice, was excellent if a little precise.

By now, we were inside a huge kitchen; pleasantly old-fashioned, I thought at first, noticing the stone flagged floors covered with coarse, rush matting, the open-backed dresser against one wall, the tall settles drawn up beside a vast fireplace in which a side of bacon hung. And then I saw the wood-burning stove inside the inglenook, the big, shining cooker beside it and the long, cherry-red curtains that must conceal a picture window looking out to sea. The room had obviously been recently and tastefully modernised.

" A chair for the young lady, Marcel! Quickly, mon petit!"

'Mon petit', taller, if anything, than Greg, quickly thrust forward a capacious, beautifully carved rocking chair, plentifully cushioned and I sank gratefully down. My ankle, by now, was causing me considerable pain.

"And you, Robert! Bring in the boy and shut the door! For July, it is exceedingly draughty!"

" My dear Tante, the English, as you should know, are accustomed to draughts!"

My annoyance at this remark was tempered by the realisation that, if Tante Jeanne was Robert's aunt, then Marcel must be his son.

For the first time, I really looked at him. The next moment, my ankle was forgotten and I was leaning forward in my seat, my fingers digging into the arms of the chair, my mouth shamelessly open. It was as well that the tall, dark man was occupied with shutting the door as he was bidden.

For I might have known that this enchanted castle would hold my grand seigneur!

And then I saw his expression of cool disdain, with not a trace of recognition, and found it hard to believe that this was the same person who had shown such consideration towards me on the previous night.

" Brandy!" Tante Jeanne was now commanding urgently. " Robert, some brandy for this poor child. Marcel, get your father a glass."

"Brandy? A cup of tea would be more suitable surely?"

Did he consider that good French brandy would be wasted on an English philistine? Or did he think me too young for matured spirits? The combination of long, fair hair, high cheekbones and freckled, retroussée nose often led strangers to think me not much older than Greg. I glanced down at my tired jeans and navy skinny-rib sweater and gave him the benefit of the doubt.

I looked up and took the full force of his inscrutable, bright blue gaze. So, his sweater *had* matched his eyes!

And then I became aware that he was standing there, waiting for me to speak. "So what will it be?" he asked impatiently. "Brandy or tea?"

I struggled to my feet. I wanted neither his brandy nor his tea . . . Nor his quite insufferable condescension!

"If," I suggested in a sort of trembling falsetto, "you would be kind enough to bring in my brother's luggage from the car; I'll drive on and leave you to your night's sleep. I'm only sorry to have disturbed you!" I took a step forward to prove my intention and my treacherous ankle immediately gave way.

'The original, crumpled heap' was how Greg described my sudden and dramatic collapse, when he saw me next day. All I remembered was the ground rushing up to meet me and those blue eyes coming nearer and nearer until I sank gratefully into oblivion.

TWO

Light, subdued but persistent, woke me. There was a dryness in my mouth. Hadn't someone, a century or two ago, offered me a cup of tea? I opened my eyes and saw, like a miracle, a cup of steaming liquid only inches away from my nose.

I lay, I discovered, in a small, silken room made by the peach coloured curtains of a massive, four-poster bed. The embroidered, satin bed cover and sheets were peach-coloured, too. I glanced quickly down at myself and was relieved to see the familiar yellow cotton of my night-dress. Who had put me into it on the previous night? I had only the haziest recollection of being carried up many steps and along a dark corridor.

Heaving myself up in bed so that I could lean against the—inevitably—peach satin headboard, I felt a twinge of pain from my ankle; now, I was relieved to discover, wrapped in a firm but comfortable bandage.

I reached for the cup and took a large, grateful sip.

"Ugh!" the brew was bitter and almost milkless. Nostalgically I thought about the cup my mother would have made. And then, the bed curtains were twitched back and Tante Jeanne's long, bony face peered through the gap.

"I thought I heard you!" Her face fell as she saw the

expression still on mine. " Your tea? It is not to your liking?" I opened my mouth to try and reassure her but she had rushed on. " No, do not bother to say anything. I have told Robert that it is just one more reason why we must have help with our English visitors."

What English visitors, I wondered sleepily.

The offending cup was now being removed. " A cup of coffee, perhaps? That, I *do* know how to make."

I nodded gratefully. " That would be marvellous, madame. I like it as much as tea."

" Stay there, then, ma petite. I will be back in one instant."

I certainly had no wish to do other than I was bidden. I lay back on the pillows and gazed through the gap in my bed curtains. By leaning forward slightly, I found I could actually see the sea, the sun already high above it. I glanced at my watch and was appalled to see that it was nearly eleven o'clock.

This was terrible! By now, I should have been well on my way . . . I threw back the clothes and carefully put my feet to the floor. My bedroom, I could now see, was vast. Long stretches of highly polished floor scattered with bright, hand-made rugs, set off to perfection the pieces of heavy, wooden furniture—the book-cases, the carved oak chest in the window alcove, the panelled wardrobe and tall, mahogany chest of drawers, set with silver brushes and combs. Through an open door, I could see into a bathroom where towels were piled beside a large, old-fashioned bath.

" Tiens! You should not be out of bed! That ankle must be rested!" My hostess was back with a cup of fragrantly steaming coffee. Protesting feebly, I allowed myself to be shoo-ed back into my comfortable bed. At least, while I drank my coffee, I should be able to thank my hostess for her hospitality.

"Madam Montarial, you are too kind! I must not be of any more trouble to you!"

"What nonsense the child talks! It is I who must apologise. Forgetting the date of your brother's arrival, like this, so that you have to arrive, like a tradesman, at the back door."

In England, I assured her, it was customary for everyone to use the back door. I was not in the least worried. "My brother?" I enquired. "Is he all right?"

"Perfectly," she assured me. "At this moment, he is out with Marcel, emptying the lobster pots. We have several out on the rocks that can be reached only by boat. Robert is with them, too, so we have the place to ourselves. We can talk without fear of interruption." I looked at her expectantly. Clearly, it was more than a conventional chat she had in mind. "But first, I must ask—how does your ankle feel this morning?"

"Much better, thank you, madame, now that it has been bandaged. Who . . . ?"

"Robert, of course!" she interrupted enthusiastically. "He is good at these things. Away from civilisation as he so often is, he has become very independent and capable."

"Away from civilisation?" I repeated curiously.

"Yes. Robert writes books. Travel books about remote areas, forgotten tribes and their cultures, animals that are threatened with extinction. Always a lost cause that he delights in rescuing. And now it is his own home. This summer will be the first he has spent at Saint Pierre since he inherited the dukedom."

So, my grand seigneur was also 'le Duc'! I think I'd known it when I'd recognised him in the kitchen last night.

"He is staying at Saint Pierre," his aunt was continuing, almost as if she were reciting a prepared speech, "because it is necessary to open the château as an hotel and, in a week or so, we are expecting our first guests. English guests."

"What a splendid idea!" I said enthusiastically. "Believe me, madame, no one could have been more comfortable than I was last night."

"Bon! Now, my dear, I have a little suggestion to make. Obviously, you will not be fit to drive your car for several days. No, please let me finish!" For I had made an instinctive gesture of protest.

"It is Robert's opinion that this is so, and he knows about these things. You will only do your ankle irreparable harm if you overtax it during the next day or two."

"But, Madam Montarial, I cannot presume on your hospitality indefinitely."

The shrewd, dark eyes under the cloud of fine, silver hair twinkled at me disarmingly. "I am delighted to hear you say so, my dear. For there is no need to presume. You can, if you wish, be of infinite service to us."

"But how, madame?"

"I will tell you." Tante Jeanne smoothed the skirt of her neat, blue linen dress as she chose her words carefully. "You have already observed that our tea is terrible?" Endearingly, she pronounced it 'tereeble'. "There must be many other ways in which we are also terrible as far as the English are concerned. Robert has spent much time in your lovely country. But even he does not know how to make tea! And he will be concerned, anyway, with the running of the estate, the provision of wines for our guests, advice about fishing, sailing and the enjoyment of our lovely countryside. He is not interested in the organisation of the château from a housekeeper's point of view. I am in desperate need of someone like you. Young, enthusiastic, charming! Why not stay here for the summer and be my right handed man?"

In spite of the impossibility of the suggestion, I found myself smiling at her affectionately. She was such an enthusiastic, charming, youthful person, herself! But I must harden my heart against her ridiculous ideas.

" Madame, I am expected in Grasse. My boy friend is joining me there in a day or two."

Her face fell. " Ah, I had not realised there was a man! But, of course, with someone of your attraction, there will always be a man. Many men!"

I grinned. " Don't you believe it!"

She brightened. " This boy friend? You do not intend to marry him?"

It was my turn to shrug. " Perhaps. I don't know yet."

" In that case, a little time apart in which to assess your true feelings for each other may be exactly what you need."

" Madame, you are incorrigible!"

"Please! Tante Jeanne, not this horrible 'Madame!'" She suddenly leaned across and put her hand over mine. " Please, my dear, say that you will stay and educate me!"

I gazed at this very articulate, obviously highly intelligent woman. "I'm sure I couldn't teach you anything, Tante Jeanne," I said humbly.

"Except perhaps how to make tea!" She grinned at me wickedly. "But I do not express myself well. It would be better to say that I could not help but learn from you."

"And what would your nephew have to say about it?" I asked.

She ran her fingers through her hair so that it stood up like a halo around her dainty head—a gesture I was beginning to recognise. "Robert is being very difficult. I have told him that we must make money out of the château or we shall not be able to afford to live in it. And this he understands. But he does not want an English girl living here. And this *I* can understand. But does he require, I ask him, that we should put on the brochures, 'English girls not allowed'? As if they were dogs! Oh, mon Dieu!" Her hand was to her mouth, her face a picture of comic dismay. "I have done it again! Put in my foot, up to the knee! Both of them! You must understand, my dear, that I adore the English. It is just that Robert," she shrugged, "... well, it is a long story. Perhaps one day ..."

"Please, Tante Jeanne, think nothing of it!" I was torn between amusement, embarrassment and a certain, natural curiosity about Robert's antipathy towards English girls.

"But I have told him," she continued firmly, "that I am quite unable to manage here without someone to help me. Not as far as domestic help is concerned, of course—there are many men and women living nearby who will come to cook and clean and look after the guests. Good, kind people whom I have known all my life. No, it is someone like you, with whom I can discuss the requirements of the English guests. Someone," she gave me a sudden, gamin grin, "with whom I can enjoy a good gossip from time to time! And there is, of course, another very good point I have not made yet. As a teacher, you are not expected back at work for many weeks. Is that not so?"

I stared at her. "How did you know that I am a teacher?"

She laughed. "Your delightful brother, Gregory. And he offered the information entirely of his own accord."

"And did he happen to say *what* I taught?"

"No. That, I must admit to asking myself. A teacher of home economics. Could anything be anything more suitable?"

"*Home*," I said, laughing, "not castle!"

"But an Englishman's home *is* his castle, I have always understood!" She crowed with delight at this neat capping of my argument. "Now, before you can say no, I will leave you to dress. May I suggest that if you feel strong enough, you should then come downstairs? I will not take you on a grand tour of the château until your ankle is quite better, but you will be able to see a little of it between here and the terrace, where Robert should be, by now. He will be delighted to pour you an aperitif before lunch."

"Thank you." The thought of lunch, after my lack of breakfast, was most appealing.

I dressed quickly in navy denims and a white blouse, tucking a scarf of scarlet cotton into the neck.

"Most attractive," commented Tante Jeanne, whom I found waiting for me outside my bedroom door. Glancing to the left, I saw steep stone steps curving around a thick, central column and leading up into what was clearly one of the pepper-pot towers.

"That," said Tante Jeanne, "is the quickest way to the kitchen but you and I will take a longer but easier route. Come!"

She led me along a broad corridor where sunlight, piercing the narrow windows, lay across the carpeted floor in a trellis of light and shade.

I glanced through one window and found myself looking down into the courtyard. The Crate, I noticed, had been moved into the shade of an archway leading to a block of stables or garages. Beyond, I caught a glimpse of an orchard where donkeys browsed beneath the apple trees.

"There have been donkeys at Saint Pierre for centuries," Tante Jeanne remarked, following my gaze. "We are very proud of them."

"Enchanting creatures!" Indeed, the whole of the château, in the bright light of day, seemed enchanting. Portraits hung on the passage walls, presumably of Robert's ancestors, and tendrils of honeysuckle nodded in through the open windows. At the end, the passage joined another at right angles and, for the second time in twenty-four hours, I found myself pausing to appreciate the beauty of the scene in front of me.

I was gazing down into a sort of miniature baronial hall. On the opposite wall, crossed swords and pistols had been arranged on the cream washed stone, around shields of highly polished steel. Beneath them, a huge refectory

34

table, shining with the patina of centuries, reflected a massive silver candelabra holding long scarlet candles. And about the table stood straight-backed chairs, oak framed with seats of plaited rush. An inglenook, itself the size of a small room, held massive fire dogs and a copper bowl of yellow roses. Immediately below us two stairways, balustraded with wood carved into the likeness of a leafy vine, curved graciously upward to meet on the landing where we stood. On either side were passages identical to that along which we had just come. We must, I thought, be at the centre of the building I had first seen under the stars on the previous night.

I glanced upwards to a plaster ceiling, crossed by beams and studded at their intersections with freshly painted, enamelled crests.

" You like it?" Tante Jeanne enquired anxiously.

" *Like* it! Tante Jeanne—it's superb! One of the loveliest rooms I have ever seen."

She looked pleased. " Good!" As if to let the beauty of the hall speak for itself, she said no more but led me carefully down the right hand stairway, turned to leave the massive courtyard door on our left and guided me through a small, cheerful, sitting room where chintz covered armchairs stood beside tables littered with books and magazines, and out on to a terrace, facing the full beauty of the sea. I had a swift impression of a rock spattered coast line, pounded by breakers and of a tiny island separated from the mainland by a narrow channel of foaming sea.

And then a figure rose from an iron, garden chair and crossed to a table that held an assortment of bottles and glasses.

35

"What will you drink?" enquired Robert, Duc de Montarial.

Repressing a wicked impulse to ask for tea, laced with brandy, I chose a long vermouth and soda and perched myself on the edge of a low stone wall. Glancing idly down at what I had expected to be a garden in the formal, French style, I was suddenly transfixed by the sight of a tiny beach at least two hundred feet below, at the base of a terrifyingly steep, cliff face. Hurriedly, I drew back and transferred myself, unobserved, I hoped, to the safety of a nearby chair.

"Actually," came Robert's amused drawl behind me, "it's not as sheer as it looks! There's quite a reasonable track."

I might have known that nothing would escape him! And then I became aware that Tante Jeanne must have excused herself and left us, no doubt to discuss her 'project' on our own.

Robert brought my drink and took a chair opposite mine. Covertly, I studied him. He wore a navy, towelling shirt over pale, linen trousers and looked altogether more friendly than on the previous night.

"You slept well?" Only by the slightest of accents would a stranger have known that English was not his mother tongue.

His eyes above the rim of his glass seemed to show a genuine concern for my welfare. But then, the Duc de Montarial would naturally show a certain courtesy towards any guest under his roof. From a personal point of view, it didn't mean a thing.

"Very well, thank you." I was equally as polite.

"And the ankle?"

" Still a little painful but much more comfortable. I understand I have you to thank for bandaging it."

He shrugged. " It was nothing." He suddenly fixed me with his brilliant, blue gaze. " I gather my aunt has made a suggestion to you about how you should spend the next few weeks of your holiday. I hope you have realised, Miss Purvis, that my aunt is an extremely persuasive person. Sometimes, it is necessary to be very strong minded when asked to do something quite impossible. Like altering one's entire holiday programme at a moment's notice."

He certainly doesn't want me to stay, I thought; and immediately felt a childish impulse to defy him.

" I have reminded her," he continued, " that I already have sufficient knowledge of the English way of life to satisfy any requirements of our guests."

I let that pass. " I think she may also wish for some feminine company, too," I pointed out.

He glanced at me sharply. " That is nonsense! I have several woman friends who are regular visitors to the château."

I thought of the disdainful looking, blonde beauty I had seen sitting in the passenger seat of his car and thought it likely that Tante Jeanne would not welcome her as a confidante. " *Your* friends," I pointed out coldly, " may not necessarily be hers."

He frowned. It was an impertinent observation on my part and for a moment I thought his tongue would lash me with the words I richly deserved. But then his brow cleared and he said, mockingly,

" And what about *your* friends? Surely they will expect you to join them as soon as your ankle is fit

37

enough for driving?"

"Don't worry!" I said. "I wouldn't dream of trading on your hospitality a moment longer than is necessary." And that, I thought to my annoyance, is precisely what he intended me to say! However much I might like his aunt, I was finding *him* quite insufferable.

And then, Greg and Marcel, towels under their arms, hair still wet from the sea, climbed up on to the terrace, presumably from that precipitous cliff. The rapport between the two, I was delighted to note, was already very apparent.

Boy-like, Greg went immediately to the point, "Tante Jeanne says you may be staying for a while. That'll be super!"

"I, too, would be delighted," said Marcel gallantly.

He was a tall, thin, fair boy, not in the least like his father.

"You see," said Tante Jeanne triumphantly, coming out on to the terrace in time to hear this last remark, "everyone wants you to stay!" Suddenly I knew what I was going to do.

"Not everyone, I think," I said, carefully avoiding looking at Robert. "But I will accept a majority vote. Thank you very much for the invitation, Tante Jeanne. I will stay, at least until your first guests arrive."

After all, perhaps Tante Jeanne had been right about Nigel and me. Perhaps a little game of 'hard to get' was just what was needed at the moment. In a day or two, I would telephone the villa at Grasse and tell him of my change of plans.

"I hope," said Robert, smooth as silk, "that you will not regret your choice."

I felt a tingle of apprehension. It was, I knew instinctively, well within this man's power, to make or mar my 'working' holiday. I, too, hoped that I would not regret it.

THREE

Lunch was something of a festive occasion; almost as if Tante Jeanne had known that I would agree to stay on at the château.

We ate on the terrace, the boys carrying trays from the kitchen and Robert going underground to return with a bottle of some delicious white wine that we drank chilled; the perfect accompaniment to the lobster with its piquant sauce that seemed to contain more than a dash of Robert's brandy.

Tante Jeanne had a sudden thought. " You like sea food, Sally and Greg? It does not disturb your stomachs?"

We reassured her quickly.

" You can at least be certain of good sea food during your stay," said Robert, as if there were some aspects of it he certainly couldn't recommend. But his manner towards me had undergone a subtle change and I began to relax; it was as if, once my decision to stay had been taken, he had resigned himself to the inevitable and was at least going to be hospitable.

" The mussels that we pick on Les Roches when the tide is out," he gestured towards the little island out in the bay, " are quite delicious. A speciality of the house, you might say."

He glanced at his watch. "Another couple of hours and you can walk to the island comfortably, as long as you don't mind getting your feet a little damp. Not," he advised hastily, "that you should undertake such a long walk at the moment, with your bad ankle."

"Perhaps I could go on my day off," I said, thinking it best to establish that I was staying for a specific purpose and expected no favours from him. "Or my half day," I amended, thinking that I would hardly be here long enough to justify a whole day off.

He made a comic grimace at his aunt. "You had better give Miss Purvis a full list of her duties as soon as possible, Tante! With hours of commencing and finishing work!"

Tante Jeanne, however chose to take the matter seriously. "Indeed, yes, Robert! You are right. This is something to which I had not given sufficient thought."

"On the other hand, Tante," Robert continued, now clearly enjoying himself at my expense, "Miss Purvis has only agreed to stay until our first guests arrive. Until then, she will be here in a purely advisory capacity, so the question of working conditions does not really arise."

"But perhaps she will be so enraptured by the Château of Saint Pierre that she will decide to stay longer," Tante Jeanne suggested. "It must be our concern to make her happy."

"If I may," I interrupted, "I will telephone to Grasse in a day or two, to explain why I haven't arrived."

"Yes, of course," said Tante Jeanne. "Your gentleman friend will be worried."

I sincerely hoped she was right. But any doubts I

might have on the subject, I certainly intended to keep to myself.

"This gentleman friend," Robert pursued, "may I ask if he is your fiancé?"

"Not yet," I said coolly, "but it is only a question of time."

"As are most things," he assured me solemnly. "Marcel, I have just had a brilliant thought."

"You have, papa?" They exchanged small, conspiratorial smiles and I guessed that there was a very close relationship between them.

"You remember the invalid chair Grandpère constructed when your Great Aunt Louise came to stay?"

"Yes, papa. It is in the stables."

"Do you not think it would be the ideal vehicle for taking Miss Purvis on a grand tour of the grounds after lunch?"

Marcel nodded enthusiastically. "An excellent idea, Papa!" He turned to Greg. "It is very easy to push."

Greg grinned at me. "Back to your pramhood days, Sal!"

I smiled back, a little feebly. I wasn't at all sure that I welcomed the idea of being pushed around by two vigorous teenagers, but I supposed it was kind of Robert to think of it.

"Robert!" Tante Jeanne addressed him decisively. "I am sure that Sally would prefer to be addressed by her delightful Christian name, rather than this formal 'Miss Purvis'. She is already calling me 'Tante Jeanne'."

Robert looked at his aunt affectionately. "In England, my dear Tante, you would be known as the original

Universal Aunt! But you are quite right!" He turned to me and gave a formal little inclination of his head. "Sally! I am enchanted to make your acquaintance! And you, I trust, will call me Robert. I hope, too, that your stay with us will be a happy one."

I felt a childish blush creeping up my cheeks. It was idiotic to feel so pleased that my 'grand seigneur' occasionally behaved according to plan. In my confusion, I bent my head over the delicious apricot compote that had followed the lobster. I turned to my hostess. "Tante Jeanne, you are a superb cook but surely you will have help when the visitors arrive?"

"Indeed, yes! My dear, faithful Marie-Claude, whom I trained myself when she was little more than a school-girl. Although I shall relieve her, of course, when she has the need to rest."

"I, too, would be very happy to take my turn," I assured her, "if you would allow me to."

Her face creased into a broad smile. "I, too, would be more than happy," she said, "since that would mean you would still be with us!"

I bit my lip. Was it a mere slip of the tongue or did I, deep down, want to stay indefinitely in this delightful château where my enigmatic host was the only possible fly in an otherwise perfect ointment? I would be guided, I decided, by Nigel's reactions when I eventually got him on the telephone.

If he seemed displeased at my decision, then I would leave as soon as I decently could. But if not—then I would reconsider.

Luncheon over, Marcel took Greg away to look for my 'pram' and Robert, too, stood up.

" If you will both excuse me? Unfortunately, I have a prior engagement." He turned to Tante Jeanne. " I had already promised to take Denise for a sail. I trust," the blue eyes seemed far too innocent as he looked at me, " that you will have an enjoyable afternoon, Sally."

Tante Jeanne looked after him ruefully as he went into the house. " Denise Dumas is the daughter of our neighbour. She and Robert have known each other since childhood."

She left it at that but something about the pre-occupied way in which she scattered the crumbs from the table to a pair of white doves that had suddenly materialised on to the parapet, suggested that she was worried.

I hobbled after her through the little sitting room, across the hall and down a short passage to the kitchen. There, I was introduced to Thérèse, the daughter of Marie-Claude, a slim, dark-haired girl who gave me a shy smile before going back to the dish washer, housed in a little scullery off the kitchen.

" Thérèse comes in every morning," Tante Jeanne explained. " She lives with her parents at the lodge, ' Les Quatres Vents ', where Marcel and I stayed until Robert came home and we decided to open up the château to visitors."

" So that must have been Marie-Claude to whom we spoke last night," I said, pleased to be able to add to my small store of local knowledge.

" That is right. We exchanged houses, in a way, since Marie-Claude and Pierre have been caretakers of the château for the last couple of years. They lived in the little flat over the stables where Robert sleeps now."

44

I thought of the heated discussion about the Montarials in the village crêperie last night, and wondered if I dared to probe further into the family history. But it would be presumptuous to do so, I decided, and said no more.

The boys came back, pushing an ancient and thickly cobwebbed invalid chair; at least, Greg was pushing, Marcel was riding, bowing graciously to an invisible audience as he came. It was *that* sort of a vehicle! More a carriage than a chair, with a sort of long, curving rudder-like contraption rising in front of the occupant.

" I *think*," Greg suggested, " that it may have had a motor at one time."

" It had," Tante Jeanne agreed. " Also thick rubber tyres so that one never knew when Aunt Louise was going to appear, prodding one with a very long, pointed stick!"

" Like old Farmer le Brun with his oxen!" said Marcel with a chuckle, stepping out of the chair and making to usher me into it.

" What are you thinking of?" Tante Jeanne chided her great-nephew. " Out into the courtyard with you, and brush off those cobwebs!"

The chair shot off again, propelled this time by Marcel with Greg ' at the wheel '.

" They are good company for each other, those two," said Tante Jeanne approvingly, as we followed them more slowly. " It is very good for the place to have young people living in it again."

Ridiculously, for some one who had been there for less than twenty-four hours, I, too, felt pleased. But I wondered, also, why even a temporary period of ' desertion ' had been considered necessary.

With Tante Jeanne's restraining influence upon my charioteers, I enjoyed my ride around the environs of the château. First, I was shown the formal garden where red and yellow roses were trained neatly across the south-facing wall of the château and miniature hedges of clipped box separated beds of tiny, jewel-like flowers that were impossible to identify from the terrace where I had been ' drawn-up.' Immediately beneath my feet, however, a multi-coloured profusion of bee-happy snap-dragons reminded me of my mother's more casual cottage garden.

Then I was pushed up a narrow, grass-grown track to the apple orchards where long lines of trees were already laden with half-grown fruit. I asked what was done with them.

" We have our own cider press," Tante Jeanne explained, " Operated by a water wheel. But that, we will show you on another day, as the road to the river is rough and difficult."

We came back down the track into the courtyard and made for the archway into the stables. There were windows, I noticed, in the thickness of the archway wall, with a flight of shallow steps leading up to a blue-painted door. There were tubs of petunias spilling colour against the grey stone and a fig tree spread its fleshy leaves in the angle of the walls.

" Robert's little flat," said Tante Jeanne.

Charming though it obviously was, I glanced back involuntarily at the elegance of the château. Tante Jeanne clearly followed my train of thought.

" Robert is a man of very simple tastes," she said.

46

"He prefers to live here for the time being."

Until, perhaps, he married Denise Dumas? I wondered.

The Crate still stood in the shadow of the archway. Greg gave it a friendly pat as we passed.

"I'll have to take her for a run, soon," I said, "or the battery will be flat."

"It is always possible to re-charge," observed Tante Jeanne placidly.

Just as I was being re-charged by my enforced idleness in these beautiful surroundings? Certainly, this was considerably more restful than batting down the centre of France in my ancient if beloved car.

Through the archway were neat rows of loose boxes on either side of a paved yard. A huge chestnut in its centre dappled the white rails and green doors with a shifting pattern of light and shade. A beautiful piebald horse put its head over the door of a box and whinnied softly.

"Robert's mare, Sylphide," said Tante Jeanne, patting the white blaze on the long, questing nose that found, miraculously, a lump of sugar in her pocket. "Apart from Napoleon Bonaparte, the family pony, she is the only horse we have at the moment. Napoleon is somewhere in the orchard with the donkeys."

At the bottom of the yard was a shingled dove-cot and beyond, more apple trees, but scattered haphazardly, among a tangle of unmown grass speckled with clover heads and rich with meadow-sweet. A narrow path curved to a patch of purple thistles where the donkeys—at least a dozen of the furry grey creatures—stepped delicately between the prickles. The big dark eyes stared at us soulfully and the chewing stopped for all of five seconds.

"That's Patience," Marcel identified a sturdy little animal. "And that's Pinafore next to him. They were born when Grandpère was alive and he was devoted to your Gilbert and Sullivan."

"For ten years at a time," Tante Jeanne explained, "the names begin with the same letter and then we move on, down the alphabet, so that we know roughly how old the animals are. The first was called Abraham and he was brought to the château in the middle of the seventeenth century to carry seaweed up from the beach. His wife was named Antoinette and their children were Benjamin and Berenice."

"Why don't we put Miss Purvis on to Patience and take her down to the cove?" Marcel suddenly suggested.

"Oh, I don't think . . ." I demurred hastily, remembering the terrifying drop to the shore from the sun terrace.

But, "Excellent!" said Tante Jeanne. "And I will ride Pinafore."

Greg looked at me reassuringly. "I'll walk on the seaward side of Patience, if that will make you feel any better, Sal."

"Thanks," I said gratefully. "It certainly would."

Patience and Pinafore were led inexorably away to have their saddles and bridles fitted and, minutes later, came plodding placidly back for our approval. They looked charming in dark blue, felt saddles and scarlet leather bridles with a cluster of tiny bells on the brow bands. "So that we know when they are coming," explained Tante Jeanne.

There didn't seem any chance of this particular journey passing unnoticed, I thought. We were like a royal procession as we set off, Marcel in front, Greg at my side and Tante Jeanne bringing up the rear; all that was missing was a court jester and I could have done with a little light relief! I held my reins with one hand, the pommel of the saddle with the other and hoped for the best.

In fact, the descent to the beach wasn't in the least frightening. Invisible, beneath a slight overhang, from the terrace, the path wound backwards and forwards across the rock face in a series of wide loops, giving me ample time to enjoy the beauty of the panorama ahead, also to study the rock face as I passed within inches of the hard, grey granite. Exposed, as it must be, to the searing power of the Atlantic gales, there was little vegetation, although here and there clumps of sea pinks bloomed bravely in a sheltered cranny and, directly above, a drift of poppies was a scarlet streak against the wall of the orchards.

Ahead, the tide was going out, leaving a cove of dark, ribbed sand and allowing easy access to an adjoining bay. On the other side, a headland sheltered a small landing stage built into the rocks. As I looked, a boat with a bright blue sail came skimming out from behind Les Roches, separated now, from the mainland, by only a narrow channel of turbulent water.

" There is Robert!" called Tante Jeanne. " And, look! Can you see a dog waiting patiently on the landing stage?" I could, a large, black and white creature staring fixedly out to sea. " That is Perdu, Robert's faithful hound. He rarely comes into the château—for which small mercy, I am truly grateful!—but is always to be found waiting patiently outside."

" Why is he called Perdu?" asked Greg.

" Because we found him wandering in the forest, and for days we called him ' le chien perdu '—the lost dog. Robert tried to trace the owners, of course, but it was not possible. Perhaps they were holiday makers from Paris."

" Pappa had better be quick," Marcel observed urgently, " or he will be becalmed out there."

I could see what he meant. The landing stage would soon be left high and dry by the receding tide, and out in the bay, the wind seemed to be dropping.

" Isn't there a motor on board?" I asked.

" Papa doesn't believe in such artificial aids!" said Marcel with a grin. " He thinks it more character forming to trust only to nature!"

A thoroughly British point of view! I thought to myself, but said nothing. Nor did I point out that his father might possibly wish to have his lady friend to himself for an hour or two; running out of wind while out in a sailing boat was probably equivalent to running out of petrol in a car!

But he made it. As Patience and Pinafore stepped nimbly on to the landing stage, Robert was securing his boat—*La Pipette*—to an iron ring let into the side of the cliff and at the same time coping with Perdu's frenzied welcome. Without waiting to be helped, a dark, willowy girl in navy trousers and white sweater leaped on to the landing stage behind him. It came as absolutely no surprise to discover that Denise Dumas was the girl whom I had seen yesterday, in Robert's car.

She was even more beautiful than I remembered; and her enormous violet eyes didn't miss a thing. They gave me a singularly comprehensive survey, from the crown of my extremely dishevelled head down to the toes of my dusty sandals before she gave a tiny but clearly satisfied nod and advanced towards me with her hand outstretched, not waiting for a formal introduction.

" So, the little English girl Robert has been telling me about!" Her English, of course, was excellent with just sufficient trace of a French accent to give it an appealing, husky charm.

It was easy to understand her reaction. Perched up on Patience's back, I must look all of ten years old; a challenge to no woman, let alone one as exquisite as Denise Dumas. But I made a mental note to try and redress the balance a little, if I should meet her again.

" How do you do?" I said formally and turned my attention to Robert. He was also studying me carefully.

" Marcel! I hope the ride down the cliff was not too hair-raising an experience for our English visitor?"

" No, I think not, papa."

" I wasn't at all frightened, Robert," I assured him quickly. " Not once we'd started, anyway!"

" I was wondering, papa," Marcel continued, " if we could perhaps use the donkeys regularly to take our guests down to the beach?"

" Exactly what I was wondering myself!" So, his concern had not been so much for my personal comfort but for my use as a guinea-pig for his future guests!

Even so, he lingered; in spite—perhaps, because of? —Denise's obvious impatience to be gone. " Are you taking Sally across to Les Roches, today?" he asked Tante

Jeanne.

She hesitated, looking at me. " I had thought it might be a little too far for her today. Perhaps we could all go across for a picnic soon?"

Out of the corner of my eye, I could see Denise raising her eyebrows, presumably at the idea of an outing organised for my benefit. " That would be lovely," I said smoothly.

The French girl tapped her foot imperiously on the wooden planks.

" Be patient a little longer, cherie," said Robert, without looking at her. He moved quickly from Patience to Pinafore, checking the firmness of their girths. " I would hate you to slide off on the way back!"

I glanced up at the cliff face and shuddered slightly. " So would I!"

" Ride on ahead of us, then, and we will pick up any fallen bodies we may find lying on the path!"

If it happened to be mine, I thought cynically, Denise would as soon trample it underfoot!

Robert gave Patience a firm slap on her rump and she set off obediently—and so briskly that I had to make a frenzied grab at the pommel of the saddle to prevent myself from sliding backwards. The tinkle of Denise's high pitched giggle almost drowned the sound of the donkey bells.

" Foolish creature!" I heard Tante Jeane mutter crossly. And it wasn't Patience she was talking to, I felt sure . . .

FOUR

That evening, dinner was early and eaten, very much 'en famille', at one end of the big kitchen table. Everyone, Tante Jeanne had decreed, could do with an early night.

" Me, too?" asked Robert innocently.

" You, as always, will do just as you wish!"

" Then I think perhaps I *will* follow your example, Tante. I have some paper work to catch up on, anyway." He turned to me where I sat at the table, already drowsy from the activities of the day. " What are your plans for tomorrow, Sally?"

I immediately stopped feeling sleepy and wondered guiltily, if I should be thinking of ways in which to help Tante Jeanne.

She, however, didn't seem to think there was any urgency when I enquired. " Although I must soon show you the guest list and ask your advice, Sally. I thought it possible that the region in which a person lives might help us decide on their tastes and preferences. For instance, there is a family coming from Lancashire, the centre of your cotton industry, I understand. They, perhaps, might be interested in our lace making and there is a married couple from Staffordshire, which you call ' the Potteries', I understand? A visit to the Quimper museum and pottery will be desirable, do you not think?" She stopped and gazed at me anxiously.

Such whole hearted devotion to the requirements of future guests must be rare indeed, even among the most conscientious of hoteliers, I thought admiringly. " I shall certainly do my best to advise you, Tante Jeanne," I assured her.

" Thank you, my dear! Now, tomorrow is market day in Saint Pierre. Not that it affects us greatly as most of what we require comes from the farm at Pont des Arbres. However, it is something that you should see."

" In that case," Robert intervened, " why don't I take her? And then, for good measure, on a tour of the surrounding countryside, if her ankle is up to it. It will give her some idea of how to advise our guests when they come. If, of course," he corrected himself smoothly, " she is still with us then!"

I might have been a parcel awaiting collection, for all the notice he was taking of *my* opinion!

" I think that will be an excellent idea," said Tante Jeanne, her head bent low over the coffee she was pouring so that it was impossible to see the expression on her face.

" And what does Sally think about it?" he asked.

How kind of him to consult me! " If you're sure that you can spare the time," I said tartly, " I should be pleased to accompany you."

" Why, thank you!" he said, one eyebrow raised in comic acceptance, I hoped, of the place I had put him in. He would, I hoped devoutly, be too pre-occupied with driving on the morrow, to feel any need for conversation.

Next morning, I was up early and dressed for the occasion; as much, that is, as a limited, holiday wardrobe would allow. I chose a trouser suit of crisp, dark brown linen and teamed it with a low-necked, primrose silk blouse that should be cool enough in the heat of the day, and smart enough for any restaurant to which the Duc de Montarial might decide to take me for lunch. And the trousers effectively concealed the bandage I still wore around my greatly improved ankle.

Robert, too, seemed to have taken pains with his appearance, coming across to breakfast on the terrace in a light-weight suit of French navy worn with a brilliantly white shirt that accentuated his dark, good looks.

We left in a flutter of handkerchiefs from Tante Jeanne and the boys with Perdu sprawled in the back seat of the car. It was a big, comfortable tourer and, although far from new, running sweetly. Robert spoke not at all until we were through the gates at ' Les Quatre Vents ' and heading for Saint Pierre.

" You have already been in the village, of course?"

I told him about our visit to the crêperie.

" I see !" A small silence fell while we both, presumably, remembered the circumstances of my first, disastrous appearance at the château.

Then he suddenly turned his head, gave me a brief but devastating smile and said, " I am sorry that my reactions were so impolite when you arrived. I had no idea who you were."

Quite overcome by this unexpected admission of human frailty, I, too, found myself apologising, explaining the circumstances that had led up to our late arrival and even giving an account of the wedding ceremony

55

we had attended.

He listened with obvious interest. " So you like the Breton people? That is good."

I would have gone on to expound further on the qualities of his countrymen but we were running into Saint Pierre, a village now as densely populated as it had seemed empty on my first visit.

Clustered around the walls of the grey stone church and practically filling the square were stalls displaying every variety of country produce, butter, eggs, cheeses, poultry, paté, vegetables and fruit—there was no need to look further to cater for an entire family, no matter how varied its diet. The quantity for sale seemed not to matter; even the owner of a cheese and a few pats of butter was apparently entitled to a stall, or part of one.

Behind every stall was at least one rosy-cheeked country-woman, sometimes two or three, wearing full-skirted black dresses, neatly aproned, and with crisp, white coiffes on their dark heads. In the centre of this hive of activity, sat two elderly lace makers, the bobbins clicking in the agile, old fingers as the lace pinned to the velvet cushions in their laps grew steadily larger. A little crowd, mostly of tourists and children, stood and watched them. Although replying with the utmost courtesy whenever anyone spoke to them, they could have been sitting at home in the doorways of their own cottages, for all the notice they took.

We, too, watched for a few minutes, Robert standing by my side and acknowledging the greetings of the stall holders and their customers. Clearly, everyone knew who he was but not everyone, apparently, felt themselves to be on sufficiently friendly terms to salute him.

There were several quick bobs from the older women and the touching of caps from the men, but the younger generation tended either to smile cheerfully or to treat him with a certain reserve as if unsure either of his authority, or their attitude towards it.

One middle-aged man, oozing with self importance, came bustling up. "Ah, Monsieur le Duc!" and he worked Robert's hand like a pump handle, going off into a stream of voluble French that left me breathless.

Eventually, and more, I suspected, as a means of stemming the flood than a genuine desire to include me in the conversation, Robert introduced me and explained that he was taking me on a tour of the market.

"There is still so much to see. I haven't shown Madamoiselle the fishmarket yet. You must excuse us, monsieur."

He took my arm and led me firmly away towards a large, glass-covered building behind the church.

"A very able man," he explained as we twisted and turned between stalls and people, goats and hens, piglets and rabbits, "and much concerned with the planning of the canning factory we are constructing in the village, but capable—as the English would say!—of talking the hind leg off a donkey! Even your friend Patience! And today is not for business but for enjoyment."

Frenchmen, I reminded myself firmly, were inveterate flatterers and best treated with a certain cynical detachment. But all the same, I was conscious of a small thrill of pleasure at his last words.

The entrance to the fish market was partially blocked by an old gentleman in a seaman's sweater, selling enormous mussels from a wicker basket.

"Ah, Monsieur Le Duc!" And then there followed yet another spate of words, this time in patois.

Robert listened attentively and then put back his head and roared with laughter. He turned to me.

"Georges is always trying to sell me back my own mussels! As you know, there's a particularly large and delicious variety to be found on Les Roches. If ever you hear noises in the night, don't worry. It will probably be old Georges on his donkey taking advantage of a nocturnal low tide. I've told him he can help himself in daylight any time he wants to, but it wouldn't be the same! My grandfather was very strict and would never have allowed it, and habit dies hard!"

So this was the 'Georges' I'd been confused with on the night I'd arrived at the château!

I smiled at him and he gave me a mischievous wink in return and said something to Robert. Whatever it was, Robert's face closed up like one of his own clams; saying something in patois in reply, he led me quickly away into the market.

It had the fresh, salty tang of the sea. And no wonder. Huge piles of fish of every size and shape covered the rows of marble slabs that ran the length of the building. Many varieties I did not recognise but there were sardines, bearing little resemblance to the neatly folded variety I knew, silvery mackerel and sinuous eels, pearly-pink oysters and coral shelled crabs and everywhere, countless baskets of mussels.

I turned to Robert. "Shouldn't we be getting something for Tante Jeanne?"

He shook his head. "Marie Claude will already have ridden in on Napoleon shortly after dawn! And now, if you've seen enough, shall we be going?"

I was amused to see that we left the market by another door from the one occupied by the quick witted Georges with his sly comments. I wondered if I would ever know Robert Montarial sufficiently well to ask what the old gentleman had said about me.

" First," Robert said, as he settled me into my seat, " I will show you the 'Armor', as we call it, the country near the sea. And there is no better place than the Ile de Brehat. There, the sea is always angry and Saint Pierre will seem like a mill pond by comparison. Perdu will be able to stretch his legs there, too."

We drove fast but safely, with tantalising glimpses of vast, sandy beaches fringed with pines. After a while, I dared to ask him about the grandfather who had been " very strict."

He raised a quizzical eyebrow. " Doing your home-- work for the visitors, in case you stay? Or really inter- ested?"

" I'm sorry! I really am interested but if you'd rather not talk about it . . ."

" Forgive my teasing! I like to see that English blush of yours!"

" Don't French girls blush, then?" I felt relaxed enough for repartee.

" Not much! I think it's something to do with skin texture, though, not lack of maidenly modesty! But to get back to Grandpère . . ."

" Yes, please!"

" You would have liked him. Not only was he strict, he was also methodical and efficient. And you, I suspect, are the same."

I let that pass. "And he was a good landlord?" I persisted. "He cared about his tenants?"

"Oh, passionately! As long as they did what he told them to! My father, now, was quite different."

He paused; and something about the set of his jaw and the grip of his hands on the wheel, kept me silent, unwilling to probe.

"He was in the Resistance," he said at last. "Here in Saint Pierre."

"But wasn't that terribly dangerous?"

He gave me a wry smile. "One didn't join the Resistance, little one, for a quiet life!"

"I meant, because he would have been so well known in the district."

"Yes, you're right, of course. And he could only manage it by appearing, on the surface, to be the most servile of collaborationists. Grandpère was still alive when the Germans occupied France and he was all for pulling up the drawbridge, so to speak, and fighting it out. Father, however, knew it would only be a question of time before he would have to surrender. *His* way, I am sure, was the best. But it took patience as well as great courage and many people in Saint Pierre thought that he really was working for the Germans. Public feeling towards the family was very bitter for several years. And still is, among certain die-hards."

So that would account for the difference of opinion in the crêperie on the night of our arrival. "And after the war?" I asked quietly.

"He became something of a recluse. My mother died. I was away at school, then university." the bald statements painted a sad picture. "Although he still continued to administer to the needs of his tenants, there was little joy left in life for him. And yet he wouldn't allow me to help him when I came of age. I had begun my own peculiar way of life by then—travelling for long periods, then coming home to write my books—and he knew that was the way I wanted it."

"And still do?" I dared to ask.

He considered the question gravely. "Up to a point. I know, now, that I must stay at home until we have made what you would call a 'going concern' of our hotel, but I know also that I shall want to be away on my travels again eventually." He raised an eyebrow in my direction. "Do you find that difficult to understand?"

"Not at all," I said. "I find it an eminently sensible state of affairs, as long as you come back to Saint Pierre from time to time." Perhaps I had spoken a shade primly. At any rate, he burst into sudden laughter.

"There speaks my English school ma'am!" His chuckles lasted for several seconds before he became serious again. "It is easy, mind you, to take that attitude when one is not personally involved. On the whole, women do not like to be left. Even temporarily."

"Possibly," I conceded. I wondered if that had been his own experience with Marcel's mother. "And do you enjoy being lord of the manor?" I asked. If he wanted to exchange personalities, I was more than willing to oblige.

Again, he gave the question serious consideration. "Yes—I enjoy the sense of responsibility and usefulness. Although, of course, it is much less now than in my grandfather's day. Since the war, it has been our policy to sell the farms to the tenants and now we have only one—the Home Farm up at Pont des Arbres. Jean Maroc manages it for me and does an excellent job. In any case, I am hardly the traditional lord of the manor, as you put it. I have a mongrel dog instead of a spaniel and I do not breed birds for sport. Unlike Grandpère, who was a magnificent shot and actually hunted wild boar when he was a young man. Father, on the other hand, hated all firearms. Understandably so."

For a few moments, I thought about the brave but tragic man who had been Robert's father. "A fine grandson like Marcel must have brought a little happiness into his life, surely?" I asked.

"It was not ... that simple," he said. "Veronique ..." his voice died away.

I should have known better, I realised immediately, than to have asked a question that must bring Robert's dead wife immediately to his mind. I watched the light fade from his face like the sun from the western sky and bitterly regretted my words. Without thinking, I put out my hand—a ridiculous gesture since both his were firmly on the wheel. And stayed there.

I launched determinedly into a change of subject that I hoped would not be too obvious. "I'm very pleased," I said brightly, "that Marcel and Greg are getting on so well together."

He nodded bleakly. "Yes, I am glad, too. For a boy of fifteen, Marcel is well advanced, I think. Your brother is a little older, I believe?"

"Sixteen," I said absently. For some reason, I was busy trying to work out Robert Montarial's approximate age from the meagre details at my disposal. A baby during the war and now with a fifteen year old son, he must be somewhere in his late thirties. Not for the first time, I reflected how attractive some men became as they grew older.

"Here we are!" He had stopped the car overlooking the sea. "We won't have time to visit the island today. There is too much that I want to show you inland. But you can see its beauty from here. The rock formation, by the way, is of pink granite. Come, Perdu!"

The big, black and white dog who, until then, had sat silently in the back of the car, ran round and round him in ecstatic circles.

I looked at the panorama before me and reflected that Brittany was a country of dramatic views connected by miles of beautiful but peaceful countryside. Certainly, the Island of Brehat was the most dramatic yet.

It was really two islands joined by a narrow strip of land; rugged islands of rose pink rock rising from a turquoise sea and laced with the foam of breakers racing into the bays and narrow gullies of the heavily indented coastline. It reminded me of a backcloth to some wild, Wagnerian opera.

By contrast, the interior was flat and peaceful, crisscrossed by narrow paths, with the houses standing backs to the wind, among patches of cultivation.

I gave a small sigh of pure pleasure at the sight; lost immediately, I would have thought, in the crash of waves and the sighing of the wind blowing from the sea, but Robert seemed to catch it. He bent his head so that his mouth was to my ear. "An old friend of mine has a villa over there. Some time, we will visit him."

I found myself wondering what Denise Dumas would have to say about such a suggestion. But not for long. This was a day for grasping with grateful hands; and letting the morrow take care of itself. With a distinct sense of shock, I realised that I hadn't thought of Nigel all day.

We walked until we reached a sheltering wall. " We'll have lunch along the coast at Paimpol," said Robert, " and then we'll go inland and I'll show you a little of the ' Argoat '—the country of the wood. It is just as beautiful but more placid than this." He waved a hand to encompass the enormous stretch of jagged rocks, pounded by waves like giant battering rams.

We turned and walked back to the car and again, although my ankle was causing me no pain, he took my arm over the rough tussocks of grass.

We ate delicious omelettes followed by fresh strawberries in a restaurant at Paimpol, where the curved oak beams might have been taken from an old sailing ship, broken, perhaps, on the same rocks that I had been gazing at.

Robert hadn't apparently, his countrymen's inclination towards a lengthy, midday meal; soon we were back on the road and heading inland through the twilight of dense forests and through tiny hamlets where old men nodded drowsily under the dusty shade of the plane trees or played ' boule ' on the worn grass.

Now and again, Robert would point to a cottage, knee deep in a riot of gladioli, waxy begonias and marigolds, a wayside calvary or a gnarled wisteria draping clusters of azure flowers against an old, grey wall. Occasionally, we would stop beside a church. He would leap out of the car, take my arm and lead me inside, saying enthusiastically—

" The rood screen here is magnificent!" or—

" The carving on the pulpit here is the best in France!" or—

" Tell me what you think of the stained glass."

The treasure duly admired. I would be allowed five minutes to wander at will around the church, reading the inscriptions, admiring the statues or the detail on the model sailing ships suspended by chains from the roof of the nave.

My time up, we would go quickly back to the car and the small crowd of children that had always collected. Invariably, Robert exchanged a few words with them in patois before driving away on our whistle stop tour.

I wished that the golden afternoon would never end. For today, Monsieur le Duc had become my 'grand seigneur', the man I had dreamed about, considerate, ever thoughtful and fascinating to be with.

" Poor, little one!" he said at last, " I must have given you enough facts to fill a thousand encyclopaedias! You deserve your nice cup of English tea."

" Much chance of that!" I scoffed, as much to hide my pleasure at the tiny endearment, as anything else.

" In Brittany, all things are possible."

Soon we were driving into the picturesque, old town of Dinan.

" First," said Robert," we will have our tea and visit our last church of the day, the beautiful Basilique St. Sauveur. And then, as much for Perdu's sake as ours, we will take a little walk through the old town and around the ramparts. Your ankle is not troubling you?"

But I was already out of the car and making for a café that proudly declared itself to be the purveyor of ' English Teas '.

We sat outside on the pavement between the ancient archways supporting the first floor of the old house that was almost within touching distance of the gables of the house opposite, and Robert sat back and watched with quiet amusement while I drank my tea and enthused over the delicious little cakes that came with it.

" When will Tante Jeanne expect us for dinner?" I asked.

" Hardly have you finished one meal, than you are thinking of the next! Actually, I was wondering if you might like to dine on the way home? If you are agreeable, I will telephone my aunt and explain."

" I should love that !"

" Good! I'll telephone from the café while you finish your tea. And then we will visit our church."

Ten minutes later, we entered its cool peace, lit by the rays of sunlight piercing the exquisite spectrums of the stained glass. I drew in my breath sharply; it was too beautiful for words. Neither of us, in fact, spoke, until we were out in the sunshine again and, with Perdu, walking beneath the tall trees of the Jardins Anglais. And then it was only to comment on the magnificence of the view from the ramparts down the wooded valley of the Rance.

" To pay such a fleeting visit to such a beautiful town is a criminal offence," said Robert as we got back into the car, " but today, it cannot be helped. We will come again."

FIVE

The second restaurant Robert took me to that day reminded me of an English country club. It was decorated in perfect taste, the food was superb and, I suspected, hideously expensive. We sat at a table in a window alcove and gazed out on a vista of fountains sparkling in the golden brilliance of a dazzling sunset.

We argued like old friends over the relative merits of escargots or oysters for our first course, but agreed absolutely that duck with orange sauce should follow. With it, Robert chose a bottle of Muscadet.

" You must be conversant with our local wines in order to advise our guests. That is, of course," he made the now statutory proviso, " if you decide to stay!"

I giggled, the potency of the situation as well as the wine going to my head a little. " If I do, they'll probably all turn out to be dedicated Francophiles and tell *me* what's what!"

" Don't worry! They'll be so delighted to have such a charming adviser, they'll keep it quiet!"

I made a small, probably provocative, grimace at him. And was immediately overcome at the impertinence of Sally Purvis making faces at the Duc de Montarial! It was as if we were living in a beautiful, air-tight bubble of iridiscent happiness; and Robert, I was certain, felt it too. I knew of course that it couldn't last—tomorrow, he would be back with Denise Dumas and I would be the little English girl once more—but tonight, it was enough to be dining with an extremely attractive man who, from the look in his eyes, didn't find me totally without appeal, either.

I put back my head, raised my glass and over its rim, dared to meet the bright blue gaze I had previously found so intimidating.

He raised his own glass. " I would dearly love to know what is going on in that delightful little head at this moment. Won't you tell me?"

It was as well that he didn't know! I said the first thing that came into my mind. " I was just thinking that now I know a little more about the Duc de Montarial than I did this morning, but very little about a certain writer. Not even his ' nom de plume '."

He looked at me for a long moment as if assessing my suitability to receive such information. " Jules Fleurie," he said at last. " You've probably never heard of him."

But my eyes were wide, my mouth shamelessly ajar. " But of course I have! Who hasn't, in fact, after all that publicity? Was it two years ago, now?"

" Oh, *that*!" he shrugged dismissively. " The media was desperately short of news at the time. I did nothing beyond the bounds of ordinary human compassion."

Not much! I thought. Jules Fleurie, in the course of seeking material for another travel book, had come across a remote village, somewhere in the hinterland of South America, that was being slowly decimated by an obscure disease; so weakening, in fact, that no one had mustered sufficient strength to make the long journey in search of help. Jules, with his portable radio equipment, had quickly organised a relief party and in the meantime mounted a one-man medical mission, isolating the most serious cases and working night and day to keep the epidemic under control. As a result, he had become a god-like figure to the villagers and had stayed with them for several months after the disease had been conquered. His subsequent book had become a best-seller in its line, and there was now talk of a film.

I must have been gazing at Robert Montarial with something like hero worship in my eyes, because he suddenly snapped his fingers an inch away from my nose.

" Come back to me, cherie! I'd much rather hear that you'd read something of mine for its own sake."

" Oh, but I have! The last one about the Camargue. Those beautiful photographs of the bulls and the wild white horses. Not your usual scene, I thought, but I enjoyed it very much."

He nodded. " It was the photographer's book, really. He was a friend of mine and asked me to go along to write the captions. As it was school holiday time, I took Marcel with me. He loved it."

" I'm sure he did." I smiled across the table at him, pleased for both their sakes that there was this close bond between them.

He suddenly began to talk about the countries he had visited and the places he still wanted to explore. Hardly daring to move in case I broke the spell, I listened, fascinated. It would have been difficult to say who was the most fascinating companion; Robert Montarial or Jules Fleurie.

And then he stopped abruptly, leaned across the table

and took my hand. " I'm sorry, Sally! You are too
'sympathique!' Encouraging me to talk too much
about myself. Now it is your turn. Tell me about your
life in England. The school you teach at and your
family."

It all seemed terribly humdrum, but he looked as if
he really wanted to know, so I told him about the flat in
London I shared with two other teachers; about my
parents in Cornwall with their market garden; about the
children's books I had begun to write as a follow-up to
the bed-time stories I was always telling my nephews
and nieces—the children of my older sister, Stella, who
also lived in London with her architect husband; and
about the publisher who had begun to make encouraging noises.

" But that is most exciting! You, too, a writer!" My
heart swelled with pride.

It seemed as if the delights of the day would never
end. After we had drunk our coffee, Robert glanced at
his watch and then out into the garden where the sunset
had long faded and the fountains were crystal arcs
against the darkness of the trees.

" Should we stroll for a little, while the kitchen is
kindly preparing some food for Perdu? I have told
Tante Jeanne not to wait up for us."

Had he now! That would have caused a flutter of
conjecture in her romantic heart, I had no doubt.

We walked through a door on to a terrace and
strolled the length of the fountains. And a little further;
so that we stood in the shadow of the trees.

Was it Robert Montarial or Jules Fleurie?—or just
my own ' grand seigneur? '—who put his arms around

me, brushed my hair with his lips and held me to him in a gentle embrace that still had my knees wobbling treacherously and my own arms seeking his support?

"I should not perhaps have done that, little one! Forgive me!"

With all my being, I wanted to cry out that I did not want his apologies. And that I was not a 'little one'. I was a fully grown woman, longing to stay in the shelter of his arms; my lips already parting for his kiss. But it was of no use. He was already putting me gently away from him.

"We must go back, Sally, before you catch cold."

Suddenly weary, I allowed myself to be led back beside the fountains and into the foyer of the club. There I turned to him. "Thank you, Robert, for a most wonderful . . ."

My voice died away as I saw the unbelievable hardening of his expression. For a second, I thought that my inadequate expression of gratitude had irritated him and then I saw that he was looking beyond me; at a tall, fair young man who was walking towards us, hand outstretched.

"Robert, I am so pleased to see you again. I had hoped . . ."

And then his voice, too, had faded as he met the look of cold contempt on Robert's face.

"Good evening, Duprés! Come, Sally!"

I followed him, passing the young man with a quick glance of compassion. For he looked almost unbearably distressed at the fierceness of Robert's rejection.

We travelled back to the château—a good two hours drive—in almost total silence. Who the young man was and why he had been treated with such disdain, I was not told.

My beautiful golden bubble was shattered into a thousand coloured fragments, and piercing them together was an impossible task.

SIX

Long before the sun's rays had reached my pillow next morning, a feeling of disquiet niggled me into consciousness. For several minutes, I lay watching the sapphire sea deepen to iridescent turquoise while I relived the events of the previous night.

Robert and I had reached the château just before midnight, to find everyone in bed and a short note from Tante Jeanne telling us there was coffee and sandwiches in the sitting-room. Neither of us had wanted food or drink—nor to prolong the evening. Checking meticulously that I had everything I needed, Robert had bowed mechanically over my hand and wished me goodnight. And would I please slip the catch of the front door after he had gone?

The click of the lock had seemed to stress the ending of our brief period of intimacy and I, too, had gone wearily to bed. Tomorrow, I would telephone Nigel in Grasse. Remembering this, now, I got up quickly and washed and dressed, feeling, for some ridiculous reason, like a French ' aristo ' en route for the guillotine.

Breakfast was not an easy meal. Tante Jeanne and the boys were obviously bursting with curiosity about the previous day, but I found it difficult to enthuse when my companion was sitting beside me, clearly pre-occupied with his own thoughts.

"At least, it was a change for you," observed Tante consolingly. Just as if I'd lived twenty years or more at the château, and was bored to distraction!

"And you, Robert? Did you not enjoy your little holiday?" Tante didn't give up easily.

"It was most enjoyable, thank you. And Sally was a delightful companion. And now, if you will excuse me, I must bring Sylphide in from the orchard. It is going to be a hot day and the flies will trouble her."

"May Greg and I come with you, Papa?" asked Marcel.

"Of course!"

He ruffled the boy's hair affectionately, but I had the feeling that his own company was preferable at the moment. I frowned into my coffee cup. Then glanced up to catch Tante Jeanne gazing at me anxiously. Now that we were alone, I found myself blurting out an account of the day. "It was perfect," I finished, "until . . ."

"Until?"

"Until we met this young man at the hotel. A monsieur Duprés, who . . ."

"Tiens! So he is back at Ker Jean!" Her eyes wide, she stared through me, her thoughts clearly elsewhere. When she spoke again, it was as if she were repeating a lesson, learned long ago. "It is difficult for any Frenchman to forget a dishonourable act against a member of his own family. And the Montarials have always been particularly sensitive about their honour." She shrugged, then gave me a tiny half-smile, "Perhaps one day—who knows—he will tell you about it himself."

"He seemed such a nice young man," I said, getting up from the table and beginning to clear the dishes. Prolonging the conversation was not only pointless but probably painful to Tante Jeanne. And it was not, I reminded myself, as if I was likely to be staying at the château long enough to become involved in any family feud.

"May I use the telephone?" I asked, after I had filled the dishwasher. "It is time that I rang my friend in Grasse."

"Of course. Use the one in the little sitting room. You will not be disturbed."

As luck would have it, my call was taken by Diana Thompson, a girl whom I knew well. "Sally, where are you? What's taking you so long?"

At least someone had missed me! "I'm staying with a real live duke in his family château, would you believe?"

"Some people have all the luck! Won't we have the pleasure of your company, then?"

"Well, that rather depends. Does Nigel happen to be around?"

There was a slight pause. "Ah, yes, Nigel! Hang on a minute. You might just be lucky."

Was he then, so elusive? Trying to curb my imagination, I hung on.

"Sal, still there? Sorry, love, he's just gone out in his car. And for the day, apparently."

"Who with?" I knew Di well enough to ask.

"Oh, some grotty female he's picked up with in your absence."

"She wouldn't, by any chance, be a girl called

Jennifer Carse?"

"Oh, you know about her!" The relief in Di's voice was very apparent. "Can't think what he sees in her, but there it is. Anyway, you should worry! You and your duke!"

"What? Oh ... yes! Well, thanks, Di."

"Not a bit! Where is it, by the way? This family château. In case the boy asks."

"Saint Pierre, Brittany. But he won't!" And I put down the receiver quickly because I had a sudden, urgent need to get my handkerchief out of my jeans' pocket.

It was ridiculous to feel so let down. I had known, after all, that this might happen. But to have my premonitions given positive substance by a third person, even one as nice as Di, made the situation doubly difficult to bear. I sat back in one of the big armchairs and gave myself up to the luxury of tears.

"Here! Have this one!"

A large white handkerchief was thrust into my hand to reinforce my inadequate square of cambric, and Robert Montarial stood in front of me. "Bad news?"

"N-n-not really!"

"Tante must have persuaded you to peel onions for her, then!" Casually, he picked up a magazine and leafed slowly through it while I mopped furiously at my face and then wondered what I should do with the sodden ball of his handkerchief.

"Here, let me have it!" Extraordinary, the way he knew what I was thinking. "Better, now?"

I nodded.

"Sally!" Tante Jeanne came bustling into the room.

76

" Have you finished your call?" She stopped abruptly and peered at me closely. " Sally . . ."

" . . . has just had no less than two of our Saint Pierre flies fighting a pitched battle in one of her eyes!" interrupted Robert smoothly. " She doesn't believe in half measures." He waved the handkerchief at me. " Can I put this away, now?"

I nodded once again and even managed a grateful smile.

" Good! Tante, didn't you say you were going to get Sally's views on the guest list? This seems as good a time as any."

Jules Fleurie, champion of lost causes, I thought, as Tante Jeanne crossed to a bureau then came to put a list of names in my lap. She had just sat down beside me when Greg and Marcel wandered into the room.

" Excellent!" Robert greeted them. " Just in time to join in our Guess the Guest competition! Now, Tante, if you will just read out the names and the districts they come from, Sally and Greg will tell us how they imagine them to be and Marcel can write down their forecasts. We shall then be in a position to judge later, how accurate they have been! Please begin, Tante."

" Miss Amelia Harrington from Cheshire."

I shut my eyes the better to concentrate. " I see a charming lady in her middle fifties. A school teacher. Living alone, from choice, in an old, thatched cottage with a pink, cabbage rose over the porch . . ."

" . . . and has a cat called Rufus," Greg took over. " A big tabby with a hole in one ear where he was bitten by the dog next door."

I opened my eyes to discover Tante Jeanne staring at

us in astonishment. "You mean, you are actually acquainted with this lady?"

Even Robert looked impressed and Marcel had quite forgotten his secretarial duties.

"As a matter of fact," I explained, "It's a sort of family game we play at home. Someone has to describe a person we all know, but without mentioning obvious details like colour of hair, height, etc. and the others have to guess who it is. When we were young, my parents said it was good for our powers of observation. And now, we just play it for fun."

After that, everyone had a go. Even Tante Jeanne, screwing up her face in painful concentration over Major and Mrs. Brigginshaw from Staffordshire and conjuring up a retired army officer, white of hair and brown of face, and pairing him with a doting wife who waited on him, hand and foot.

Marcel, chuckling so much he could hardly write, came up with a red-haired lion tamer and his acrobatic wife for a Mr. and Mrs. Trask, writing from London.

"Hope they leave the lions at home!" said his father, before himself going off into a trance over Rowena Herbert, who hadn't thought to mention her marital status. All we knew was that she came from Surrey. He stayed quiet for nearly a minute while the rest of us maintained a reverend hush.

"Young. Very tall, with long blonde hair that she's perpetually pushing away behind very pretty little ears. Big eyes that she has a habit of opening even wider when she wants to make a point. Rather precise, perhaps, but with a wicked sense of humour." It was as if he knew her by heart. His eyes flicked open. " Got that,

78

Marcel?"

Apart from a Mr. and Mrs. Davenport from Lancashire, we had now exhausted the list. Between us, we made Mr. Davenport into a bank manager and allowed his wife to breed Cairn Terriers and preside over the local bridge club, then turned our attention to what Saint Pierre and its environs had to offer in the way of entertainment.

" Personal attention," said Tante Jeanne firmly. " That will be the most important factor. And this should be possible with just a few guests, while we find our ... our ... " She looked at me hopefully.

" Feet!" I supplied. " And, if you still want me, I *should* like to stay on and help."

" Still want you? My child, that will be wonderful! I had hoped, of course, but ... "

" On one condition," I insisted, " that I move out of what must be one of the best bedrooms in the château and into something smaller. An attic, perhaps?"

" I am sure we can do better than that!" She thought for a moment then looked across at Robert. " There is the smaller flat over the stables, of course. That would be ideal for Sally. But I don't see how ... "

" Why not?" I asked. " It sounds super."

She looked at me reprovingly. " While Robert is there, Sally, it would not be ' comme il faut ' for you to sleep so near."

" The permissive age," Robert explained to me with a twinkle, " might never have happened as far as Tante is concerned. And nothing you can say to her, will make her change her mind. But, I wonder," he glanced across at Greg, " if her scruples would be satisfied if your

79

brother shared the flat with you. It is quite big enough for two."

"Excellent!" said his aunt. "I shall be quite happy about that arrangement. It is not, as I am sure you understand, Sally, that you and Robert are not completely trustworthy. But, where the reputation of a young girl is concerned, the proprieties must be observed."

"I appreciate your point of view, Tante Jeanne," I said meekly. "Thank you."

I was now feeling considerably more cheerful, and it was almost entirely due to Robert's tact and kindness.

The telephone shrilled and I moved to sit near Greg while Tante Jeanne answered it.

"Ah, Miss Harrington!" She raised her eyebrows at us and then continued in French. "Yes, I see." She listened for several seconds. "Yes, that will be perfectly convenient. We will look forward to seeing you tonight. At about ten o'clock? No, Miss Harrington, that will not be too late. Au revoir!"

She put down the receiver and gave me a mischievous smile. "We will soon be able to see if your imagination was correct, Sally. That was Amelia Harrington. Apparently, she is with Major and Mrs. Brigginshaw and they have been touring France together, arriving in Paris ahead of schedule. They will reach St. Pierre a day earlier than expected."

I turned to Greg. "Then we must move this morning."

"Bring the suitcases down when you have both packed, Greg, and I will take you both over to the flat," said Robert. "That will be in order, Tante?"

"Yes, except that I would like to give it a thorough

80

clean first. I wonder if Thérèse . . ."

"Please," I entreated, "let me do it. Thérèse will have enough to do, now."

"Thank you, if you are sure. I shall be in the kitchen if you need me."

Since I had never really unpacked, it took me only a few minutes to fill my suitcases. I left the largest outside Greg's door and took the other down myself. There was no one in the hall but a door stood open into a room I had not yet entered.

"Good morning, Sally! Come in!" Denise Dumas beckoned languidly from an elegant, gilt fauteuil.

I paused on the threshhold. "What a charming room!" It was a symphony in gold and green, as if inspired by the garden, clearly visible through the long, elegantly proportioned windows. Lacquered, gilt chairs and sofas, upholstered in amber silk, stood upon a pale green carpet with long curtains of watered silk combining the two colours in an irridescent sheen, lacquered cabinets in the corners and against the walls held pieces of exquisite porcelain and glass.

"Yes, the Garden Salon is one of Françoise's best achievements, I think," said Denise.

"Françoise?"

"Of course! I was forgetting you don't know Robert's family." As a method of putting me firmly in my place, the remark couldn't have been bettered. "Françoise is Robert's sister, and one of the most accomplished interior decorators in Paris. She re-designed much of the château when Robert decided on this ridiculous hotel idea."

"It is very beautiful," I said, looking around me. And

81

then, since Robert still hadn't appeared for my suitcases and I was uncertain what to say to this smooth,
silky creature, I found myself praising the beauty of an
exquisitely inlaid, mother-of-pearl box, the central fea-
ture of a collection of pearl objects set out on a table
near the door.

" Why not open it ?" Denise suggested lazily.

I did so and the opening bars of Sinding's lovely
' Rustle of Spring ' rippled through the room.

And then the door was suddenly slammed back against
the wall and Robert stood there, his face pale, his eyes
cold as marble.

" Who . . . ?" And then he saw me, standing there.
" Oh, it's . . . you."

I felt as well as heard the anti-climax in his voice.
You! Sally Purvis! Unimportant bird of passage, not
even worth the losing of one's temper.

I lifted my chin. " Yes—it's me! I'm sorry if I
shouldn't have opened the musical box." I shot a quick
glance at Denise, but she was gazing blandly over my
head.

" It's of no importance," said Robert crisply. " Are
you ready ? " But, clearly, it *had* been of importance,
reviving something from the past that would have been
better left undisturbed. And how many more ghosts was I
quite inadvertantly—to uncover? Prying or not, the
time had come for a quiet word with Tante Jeanne.

Our mews flat was charming. At right angles to that
of Robert's, it consisted of a long, narrow, sitting room,
two tiny bedrooms and a galley-like bathroom. The furniture was strictly functional and there was little to be
done in the way of cleaning, but I peered into a broom

cupboard and found all the necessary equipment.

" I'll just flick a duster around," I told Greg, once Robert had departed. " No need for you to stay."

" Suits me! Housekeeping isn't really my scene!" He leered at me wickedly, intimating, presumably, that the casinos of Europe were far more his milieu, then turned and ran after Robert.

Left alone, I abandoned all ideas of dusting for a few minutes, and hung out of my bedroom window, absorbing the atmosphere of my new home. In front of me were the branches of the chestnut tree, their sombre depths lit by the pale, prickly spheres of the forming fruit. Immediately beneath me, Sylphide had her head out of her box, watching a pair of doves peck between the cracks of the paving stones. Muted by distance and the thick walls of the chateau, the sound of the sea reached me like the soft purr of some enormous cat. I breathed in great lungfuls of air, rich with the sleepy scents of summer—honeysuckle, hay, the heady fragrance of mimosa—then turned back into the room and dreamily began to arrange my toilet articles on the dressing-table top.

Straightening up in front of the mirror, I caught myself pushing the hair back behind my ears and stood, arrested in mid-gesture, my eyes opening wide as I remembered Robert's words when describing the imaginary Rowena Herbert—' long, blonde hair that she's perpetually pushing away behind her ears . . . eyes that she has a habit of opening wide when she wants to make a point—rather precise but with a wicked sense of humour '.

Thoughtfully, I continued to arrange hair brush and

comb, suntan oil and lipsticks. Even after the shared pleasure of our day together, I couldn't delude myself into believing that I had been the first person to come to his mind when conjuring up an imaginary female.

Even more troubled, in retrospect, by the incident of the musical box, I went in search of Tante Jeanne.

SEVEN

The opportunity to probe discreetly, without, I think, rousing Tante's suspicions, came sooner than I had hoped.

Later that day, the weather holding good and the tides being convenient, she had planned a picnic on Les Roches. As she pointed out, it would be the last time that the family could be alone together, before the guests arrived.

I warmed to that 'family' which clearly included Greg and myself and happily helped pack the cold chicken, salad and cheese cake that she had prepared. Afternoon tea not being a meal that the French found necessary, lunch had been decided upon as our picnic feast, with a swim beforehand.

A little of the sparkle, admittedly, left the day when Tante informed me that Robert would not be coming. "He has to visit the farm, and Denise has decided to go with him." But on the other hand, I consoled myself, it might now be easier to discover what I needed to know.

This time, a little cavalcade of three donkeys set off— Pinafore and Patience for Tante and myself with Ruddigore, a slightly younger beast, as pack animal. With Marcel at the head and Greg at the rear, we wound our way down the cliffs and, urged on by the shouts and slaps of the ' donkey-boys ', even managed a brisk trot across the hard sand to the island.

Once there, the animals were unsaddled and left to graze while we walked round to the seaward side of the island, to a big hollow sloping upwards to a lip of sheltering rock. You could choose between lying on your stomach to study the seabirds riding the waves below or lie, basking in the sun, further down the slope, viewless but for the sky above but completely sheltered from the sea breezes.

Tante Jeanne and I elected to bask while the boys prepared to climb down to swim in a little pool, shielded from the full force of the waves by a natural, granite breakwater.

Helping the boys peel off their shirts, I stood next to Marcel for a moment, comparing my pale skin with his golden tan.

I held my arm against his. " A long way to go yet!" And then I looked up to find Tante Jeanne and Greg staring at us with rather more than normal interest.

It was Greg who put it into words. " Marcel looks more like your brother than I do, Sal!" And Tante Jeanne thoughtfully nodded her agreement.

We peered at each other more critically. True, we were both tall and fair with deep-set brown eyes. We even had the same scatter of freckles, although Marcel's nose, unlike mine, was long and straight.

I made some casual remark about it being nice to have an unexpected addition to my family, then watched both boys swing down through the rocks to the sea, before turning slowly back to Tante Jeanne.

She patted the grass. " Come and sit beside me, Sally."

"If I bear a certain resemblance to Marcel," I said carefully, once I was settled, "then I must also be a little like his mother."

"You are right." Tante also seemed to be picking her words with care. "It is not so much the face, although she was fair, also, but the body and the way that you carry it when you walk."

"Robert," I pursued, "must have also noticed it?"

"He has not said anything about it to me, but he must have done. Although, that first night you arrived here, he did not show any surprise."

For the very reason, I thought, that he had already seen me—lying asleep on the deck of the car ferry. And that, I suddenly realised, with a bitter jolt of disappointment, was why he had covered me so carefully with his rug. I had reminded him of his dead wife.

Tante Jeanne was still speaking. "It is not, perhaps, as surprising as you may think, Sally. Your resemblance to Veronique. Like yourself, she was an English girl."

I stared at her. Of course! Veronica—Veronique. As pretty a name in English as it was in French. Many things were now falling into place.

"That mother of pearl musical box in the Garden Salon. Did it belong to Veronique?"

"My dear! You didn't play it?"

I nodded miserably. "Denise put the idea into my head."

"Ah, that one! She is capable of anything, particularly if it will help her to keep Robert for herself. From a child, she has wanted him. Even when Veronique was alive . . ." Her voice trailed away and I let it go. My concern was with the living.

"Tante Jeanne," I said seriously, "do you really think I should stay? If I am so like Robert's late wife, surely it is unkind to remind him of her so often."

She gave me a sweet smile. "Child, you are very sympathique!" It was the second time in as many days that the word had been applied to me. "But I do not think you should worry. Robert cannot go through life avoiding beautiful English blondes."

I made a face at her. "English and blonde, I may be, but certainly not beautiful."

"That is a matter of opinion. Beauty, as your English poet has said, is in the eye of the beholder."

"Was . . . Veronique beautiful?" Somehow, I had to know.

A veil came down over Tante Jeanne's face. In spite of what she had told me about enjoying a good gossip, I knew she would never dream of discussing the personal affairs of others, particularly those of her own family. But she answered my questions—in a few, simple words that told me all I wanted to know.

"Very, very beautiful."

I was silent, understanding only too well, now, why Robert withdrew so often into himself—and his memories.

"Sally," Tante Jeanne broke in gently upon my thoughts, "for my sake, you cannot leave Saint Pierre now. Look at my hand!" She put out her right hand and deliberately made it tremble like an aspen leaf. "Can you believe, Sally, that the thought of meeting the efficient Miss Harrington and Major and Mrs. Brigginshaw terrifies me? Without you by my side, I would be scared—how do you say it?—out of my wit?

No!" she shook her head as I began to protest. "It is true. Remember that these are my first *paying* guests. It is one thing to invite people to stay—they come at their own risk?—but when they are actually paying, one is under a great obligation to give them what they want."

It was a point of view I hadn't considered but, in view of Tante Jeanne's conscientious attitude, very understandable. "I am quite sure," I told her, "that everyone will love you!"

"You are very kind. But, even so, I shall feel happier when today is over."

The picnic was an unqualified success and if I found myself occasionally looking to see if Robert might be walking across from the mainland, that was my own ridiculous fault.

"Your guests will love it here," I assured Tante Jeanne as the little waves began to cream across the sand and we loaded Ruddigore with the remnants of our picnic. "Just as I do."

EIGHT

Later that same day, after an afternoon of exhaustive preparations, I walked up the dusty track that led away from the sea towards the farm at Pont des Arbres. Tante Jeanne had decided that we needed more butter and I had jumped at the chance of getting away for a while.

It was strange how constrained I had felt in Robert's company since the revelations of the afternoon. Every time I felt his eyes on me, I could imagine the stab of remembered pain I must be causing him.

We had all spent a busy afternoon; Tante Jeanne and Thérèse in the preparation of an enormous Dundee cake —' to make our guests feel at home ', Tante had said, with what seemed to me a total lack of logic—Robert and the boys in grooming the donkeys and cleaning their tack, and I in putting the final touches to the guest bedrooms.

The question of suitable flowers had occupied me for some time. It was amusing how the identities we had given our guests had stayed, and even grown. Major Brigginshaw, having now, according to Tante Jeanne, retired from army life, could well have taken up the culture of roses as a pastime, and so I had arranged an enormous bowl of Gloire de Dijon in his room. A tall vase of vivid, tiger lilies awaited the redoubtable Miss

Harrington in hers!

There was nothing more to be done now, and I swung briskly up the track between elder bushes stippled with blossom. At the top of the lane, where it made a wide curve to reach a farmhouse clearly visible among the trees, was a field where wheat straw stood in neat bales among the golden stubble. I leaned on a stile and thought that if I walked carefully between the bales towards the farmhouses, I should be doing no harm.

It was only when I had nearly reached it that I realised why Tante hadn't suggested the short cut. The house didn't belong to the farm at all, but was a private residence in its own large garden. Once, perhaps, it had been an old barn but now it was a highly desirable dwelling, with blueshuttered windows let into the thick walls and the carved wooden eaves beneath the ochre tiles, silvered with age. Like a green-gold sea, the wheat field lapped the white walls, and there was no sign of a right of way that I could legitimately take. There was nothing for it but to turn back and retrace my footsteps. Strange, though, that no one at the château had mentioned the proximity of such a beautiful house.

Thinking that I must remember to tell my architect brother-in-law about it, I took one long, last look and had actually turned my back when there came the sound of a window opening and a voice cried, " Un moment, ma'amselle!"

From one of the big picture windows on the ground floor, a man was leaning out. A man whose face I recognised instantly. Last time I had seen him, he had been wearing formal clothes and now a pair of blue linen trousers were topped by a matching, open-necked shirt, but there was no mistaking the man to whom Robert had been so rude on the previous night—Monsieur Duprés.

From his sudden, startled exclamation, it was obvious that he hadn't, at first, recognised me, either. I walked slowly towards him.

"Excuse me, m'sieur," I began in my careful French. "I did not mean to trespass . . ."

He brushed my apologies away—in perfect English! "You are on your way to the farm, I expect?" I nodded. "One moment, and I will let you into the garden and that will give you easy access to the lane."

He left the window and a few seconds later, the door in the wall was opened and he beckoned me through. From inside, the house was even more attractive. L shaped, the two arms encompassed a cobbled courtyard, shaded by the leafy fronds of a tall acacia tree. The white walls, festooned with the sprawling tendrils of a luxuriant creeper, lent a cool enchantment to the gay window boxes of pink and scarlet geraniums.

"Oh, I *wish* my brother-in-law could see this! He is an architect, you see, M'sieur, who specialises in restoring older properties."

He gave me a whimsical smile. "I should perhaps introduce myself. Yves Duprés and I, also, am an architect. Naturally, I prepared the plans for this house so I am delighted to hear that you approve. Won't you come inside, so that you can give your brother-in-law a complete description?"

Put like that, the invitation was difficult to refuse. And I was not sure that I even wanted to. Whatever Robert had against this man, I felt myself responding to the warmth of his personality and the friendliness of his grey eyes.

"Sally Purvis," I completed our introduction as I followed him inside.

The whole of the ground floor was open-plan; one arm of the L given over to a lounging area with a dining alcove that looked out on to lawns and a willow shaded river bank; the other full of the most up-to-date cooking and domestic equipment I had even seen.

It was as he showed me a washing machine that looked as if it could even be programmed to sew on loose buttons, that he enquired about my reason for being here. Was I one of the first guests at the château?

I explained about bringing Greg and that I was now staying on in a sort of advisory capacity.

"An excellent idea! Madame Montarial is indeed fortunate to have the opportunity of your services." But he spoke almost absent-mindedly and his next question seemed so deliberately casual, that he had scarcely finished it before alarm bells were sounding in my brain.

"I wonder, is Robert's sister Françoise staying at the château at the moment?"

I shook my head, noticing how his fingers were playing abstractedly with a bunch of keys.

Evidently, he considered some explanation to be necessary for his enquiry. "I met her recently at the house of a mutual client and she was kind enough to say she would advise me on the interior of Ker Jean, when she was next visiting the château."

I glanced at the striking simplicity of white walls against the wrought iron balustrade of the stairway, the perfect positioning of the lamps with their huge, globular shades, and doubted if even Françoise Montarial could add much to the existing beauty of his house. But it was not my place to comment.

Briefly, I wondered if Robert's antagonism towards this apparently charming young man was based on anything deeper than friendship with his sister. I knew enough of the French way of life to realise that Robert, as head of the family, would take very seriously any claim to his sister's hand. But what possible objection could he have to Yves Duprés? Clearly, a man of intelligence and culture, he was no doubt highly successful in his profession, also. But then I remembered that Tante Jeanne, too, had been disapproving when I had mentioned our chance meeting with him at the country club.

However, I reminded myself again, it was not my concern. And the butter I had been sent for, definitely was! " I must be on my way, m'sieur."

" Can I not get you a drink before you go?"

" Thank you, but I must reach the farm while it is still light." I explained about the butter and Yves led me back into the garden and through another gateway on to the track that I should never have left in the first place. Not that I regretted the diversion!

" It has been a great pleasure to meet you, Miss Purvis. I trust we may meet again, soon." He bowed over my hand.

" I hope so, too, M'sieur Duprés."

As I went on my way, I wondered if relations had always been so strained between Robert and Yves. Situated as it was, in the middle of Montarial land, someone must have sold the place for development.

NINE

Fortunately, perhaps, I found that the Marocs were out, leaving an elderly farmworker in charge. So I was able to collect my butter in the minimum of time. With luck, no one at the château would notice that I had been away rather longer than was necessary. It wasn't that I intended to be deliberately deceitful, but there seemed no point in risking Robert's reactions by telling him of my brief visit to Ker Jean.

I needn't have worried. No one had missed me. Far too exciting an event had occurred in my absence. Tante Jeanne came bustling into the kitchen to meet me, words tumbling from her lips.

"Françoise has rung! Robert's sister! She will be with us in the morning." She took the butter from me then linked her arm through mine and led me into the sitting room. "You will love her, my little Francie. Such liveliness and charm!"

And Tante Jeanne wasn't the only one, I reflected with some apprehension, to find her irresistible. I wondered how long it would be before she was beating a path to Ker Jean. And would it be under cover of darkness or in broad daylight for anyone—including her brother —to see?

Meanwhile, Miss Harrington and the Brigginshaws

were expected. We all gathered in the Hall just before ten o'clock, a reception committee of Tante Jeanne, Robert and Denise—curiosity, I guessed, had brought her—Marcel and Greg and myself, with Thérèse hovering in the background.

"Ridiculous, really," Denise pointed out, "to stand about like this! They are not coming by train, but by car! Anything could have happened to prevent them arriving on time."

"I am sure it will be only a matter of minutes either way," said Tante Jeanne. "Miss Harrington sounded a *very* efficient person."

In fact, it was five minutes past ten when there came the sound of a car driving into the courtyard. Robert flung open the door and positioned himself on the steps, with Tante Jeanne and Denise beside him. Greg caught my eye and winked mischievously. I knew that he, too, was recalling the rather different circumstances of our own arrival; was it really only three nights ago?

He and I stood behind the Montarials, but I couldn't resist craning forward to see if our guesswork had been anything like correct.

A middle-aged, male figure emerged from the driver's seat and began to walk round to the passenger door. But Robert was before him, already helping a tiny, birdlike woman to alight. Mrs. Brigginshaw, no doubt.

I held my breath as Robert moved on to the rear door. But it had already been flung open. Out into the path of light flooding from the doorway, stepped a long-legged, slightly stooping figure, with dark hair tied back into severe bunches and spectacles flashing like a semaphore as she turned towards the reception committee in the doorway. I stared incredulously, unwilling to believe that I could have been so utterly wrong in my forecast. Miss Amelia Harrington was no more than Greg's age, a studious, be-spectacled school girl!

Her glance fell upon Greg and Marcel, seemingly turned to stone by the shock of her appearance. " Oh, boys!" she said dismissively. And I was reminded of my headmistress dealing with some particularly recalcitrant members of the junior school.

But, just as I could not have been more wrong, Tante Jeanne could not have been more accurate. Major Brigginshaw had a clipped, white moustache and a deeply tanned face; every inch a soldier. And his fragile little wife obviously adored him.

" Sorry to be late," he said briefly. " Cramp in my wrist. Old war wound. Painful."

" And he wouldn't let *me* drive," complained Amelia Harrington, " although he knows I can."

" My niece," apologised the Major, " has little regard for the law!"

At some point during the next few minutes, while we were all busy showing our guests to their rooms, carrying luggage or making tea, I passed Tante Jeanne on the stairs.

" I like your guessing game, Sally," she said innocently. " Some time, I must show you how to play it!"

TEN

I awoke to bird song in the orchard and the gentle rustling of Sylphide in her box below me. By my travelling clock, the time was half past six. It was my first, full working day; and the Brigginshaws, and most certainly Amelia Harrington, could be early risers.

Coming back from douching my face with cold water at the wash basin in the corner of my room, I was confronted by the spider plant Tante Jeanne had given me to trail from my window sill. It, too, looked as if it would benefit from a good soaking. Carefully, I put it on the outside sill, then fetched water in my tooth mug.

I had poured nearly all of it before a muttered exclamation made me glance hastily down into the yard. Something, of course that I should have done before starting the operation.

I saw two heads, one equine and quite incapable of twisting upwards, the other human, and twisting like mad. Robert's face was a comic mixture of astonishment and indignation; until he saw my own horrified expression. Then he gave me a broad grin.

As I began to stutter an apology, he suddenly went down on one knee on the paving stones, put a hand on his heart and declaimed—

" But, soft! What light through yonder window

breaks? It is the east, and Juliet is the sun!"

He delivered the whole, beautiful speech, ending with —"O, that I were a glove upon that hand, that I might touch that cheek!"

With a dramatic wave of my arm that nearly had the spider plant tumbling on to Robert's head, I replied.

"O, Romeo, Romeo! Wherefore art thou Romeo?"

For the first time, I blessed my English teacher for the reams of Shakespeare she had made us memorise.

We didn't, in fact, stop until somewhere around 'By whose direction found'st thou out this place?' When we were both startled by an unexpected round of applause. Greg, an absorbed audience of one, was leaning from his window.

"Don't" Robert told him, "expect a similar performance every morning!" He grinned up at me. "That is, if the fair Juliet doesn't mind restricting her horticultural activities in future?"

"She will," I promised. And then, suddenly remembering I was still wearing my nightdress, I withdrew hurriedly.

As I dressed, I found I was humming softly to myself. Life in the stableyard suited me admirably, I decided.

Leaving Perdu lying under the chestnut tree, the three of us started to walk across to breakfast together. I say 'started" because, half way across the courtyard, Robert glanced up from discussing the Elizabethan theatre with Greg, and noticed the little red sports car drawn cheekily up at the front door.

"Fran's here already! Come and meet my little sister, you two!" And the next minute he was sprinting up the steps and in at the front door.

By common consent, Greg and I continued walking round to the back door. " If his sister's half as nice as he is," said Greg, " I shan't complain."

" You my lad," I remonstrated, " should stick to your own age group."

" If you mean Amelia Harrington, by that," he gave a theatrical shudder, " she's ninety-two, if she's a day!"

I knew what he meant. I hoped for her own sake, that Amelia would soon produce some normal, teenage attributes.

We walked as unobtrusively as possible into the kitchen.

" Ah, *there* you are!" Charmingly, Tante Jeanne introduced us as 'our friends from England' and I found myself shaking the hand of a girl whose beauty had an unusual, vibrant quality. It was not so much beauty in the conventional sense of the word—her nose was almost as retroussé as mine and her chin a little too determined for perfection—but her face seemed lit by a rare, inner radiance that was enormously attractive. Her short dark hair was flicked smoothly across a broad brow and her eyes were of the same penetrating blue as her brother's.

" I am enchanted to make your acquaintance, Sally. I trust I may call you that? And Greg, too, of course." She gave my susceptible brother a ravishing smile before turning back to me. " My aunt has told me how kind you have been, even changing your holiday plans to help her."

" I could not be happier," I assured her. And a small, independent piece of my brain registered the astonishing fact that I was speaking the absolute, un-varnished truth. Jennifer Carse, or no Jennifer Carse, I had no desire whatsoever to be in Grasse with Nigel.

" I agree with you that there is nowhere quite like Saint Pierre." She stretched her arms wide as if to en-compass the entire château with its gardens and orchards. Although she wore the simplest of matching denim jacket and blue jeans, I noticed that they were of im-maculate cut, fitting her excellent figure to perfection.

" I am surprised that you remember it!" said Robert. " It is so long since you have visited us." He was obviously very attached to his younger sister, who must have been around my own age, although with that gamine quality that is impossible to associate with actual years.

" I have been so busy! Anyway, my dear brother, you are hardly the one to accuse *me* of neglect." But she crossed the kitchen to put her arms around him where he stood, leaning against the stove. It seemed a spontaneous gesture of affection, but was it also a way, I wondered, of hiding her face from him as she asked her next question?

" And where have you put me to sleep, Tante? I expect that my usual room is needed for your guests."

" I have prepared the spare bedroom in Robert's flat for you, Francie. It is very pleasant out there, is it not, Sally?"

" Heavenly!" I assured her quickly, but noticing the momentary pucker of Françoise's smooth brow. Was it because of the difficulty she would have in getting away to Yves without Robert seeing her, or the storm of protest she might expect to meet on her return? I doubted very much if Robert had shaken off his sense of responsibility towards his sister at the same time that he had begun to dispose of the Montarial estate.

What could be the outcome of such an affair? Noticing the directness of her gaze, her forthright manner, I found it difficult to imagine Françoise capable of deception. Just as it was impossible to imagine any man easily relinquishing his claim upon her affections. And Yves Duprés had not struck me as a person who would give up easily.

I must have shivered slightly for Tante Jeanne said, " Come and sit down, Sally, and I will pour you some coffee. Greg, perhaps you would go and rouse Marcel? He does not yet know that his favourite aunt has arrived."

I cupped the bowl of hot coffee gratefully while I drank, then buttered myself a croissant from the golden pile in a big, wooden dish on the table. Breakfast was obviously going to be a very informal meal at the château, now that the guests had begun to arrive. Tante Jeanne sat opposite me and absent-mindedly started to crumble a roll.

" I'll take the Brigginshaw's early morning tea up, in a few seconds, shall I, Tante Jeanne?" Amelia had scorned the suggestion on the previous night, but her aunt and uncle had obviously been delighted at the idea. They, Tante Jeanne now reminded me, were the couple who lived in the Potteries so perhaps they would like to take a trip to Quimper?

" I'll ask them after their breakfast," I promised. " Although I have the feeling they may have done enough travelling during the last week or two to last them for a while."

I was right. When I went out to see them on the patio where Thérèse had served their breakfast, I found that Amelia had already eaten and departed.

"Poor child!" said Mrs. Brigginshaw unconvincingly. "I'm afraid she finds us rather dull company."

Tactfully, I trusted, I said I thought that most unlikely but that Amelia had certainly struck me as a very active young person.

"Active!" said the Major, getting to his feet and drawing out a chair for me. "She's like an army of ants and a battalion of beavers all rolled into one! At this very moment, she's probably re-organising the local gendarmerie!"

"It's not," her aunt assured me, "that we're not extremely fond of Amelia. We'd always promised her a holiday in France the year she did her ' O ' levels. But, really," she shook her head, " It's she who's taken us!"

"The basic trouble," the Major contributed, "is that we don't speak the lingo. And she does. Like a native. Really, she's had us at her mercy."

"Well, there's no need to worry any more on that score," I said comfortingly. "Everyone at the chateau speaks perfect English. My brother and I *are* English. And more English guests are due to arrive tomorrow."

"That's marvellous!" said Mrs. Brigginshaw, with heartfelt gratitude.

I sounded them out about Quimper. "Perhaps, one day . . ." said the Major courteously. But his wife raised a languid hand, and murmured,

" All I want to do, my dear Miss Purvis, is to sit on a beach, if it's not too far away, and bask in the sun."

"That's easily arranged!" I got to my feet. "And we'll even organise transport. Come and see, if you've quite finished breakfast."

As we crossed the courtyard towards the stable archway, Amelia's voice came floating out to greet us. "I tell you, you idiots, you've *got* to have a timetable. I've already inspected the cliff path. What happens if Patience meets Pinafore on one of those S bends?"

I heard the Major draw in his breath and quickened my pace. We found Greg and Marcel standing, heads bent, by the orchard gate with Amelia perched above them. Even the donkeys seemed to be drawn up in ranks behind her, awaiting review.

She saw us coming and was off the gate and walking towards us before the boys had even turned around.

"I've been telling them, Miss Purvis, that we shall have to have a timetable once the donkeys get busy."

There was something about her tall gawkiness, the earnest eyes behind the big round spectacles, the way her hair was scraped back tightly above her cars, that I found strangely endearing. Behind that dictatorial exterior there could be an extremely shy and sensitive adolescent, trying to make human contact. Not that you could expect two male contemporaries to appreciate it!

"It's a good idea in theory," Greg conceded, "but I think we should wait until more guests arrive and we have some idea of their requirements. Anyway," he added, rather spoiling the good sense of this opinion by a childish 'red herring', "they're Marcel's donkeys!"

"Donkeys," came Robert's voice behind us, "belong to no one except themelves." He put Françoise's suitcases down on the stairway up to his flat and led his sister across to us. When she had been introduced, I explained the Brigginshaw's need for peace and quiet.

" I thought a visit to Les Roches might be in order?"

" An excellent idea!" He considered Amelia and her uncle and aunt for a moment and then glanced at his watch. " If," he said to the Brigginshaws, " you could be ready to leave in half an hour, I could even guarantee complete isolation for at least four hours. The island is cut off by the tide for that time."

" Truly?" Mrs. Brigginshaw's relief was very apparent.

" Truly! Sally will arrange packed lunches for you and we'll take care of Amelia, won't we, boys?"

I agreed to my part of the arrangement with enough enthusiasm, I hoped, to conceal the boys' obvious lack of it. But there was no doubting the Brigginshaw's pleasure at Robert's neat segregation of young and old for the next few hours. And, from the look of patent adoration Amelia was giving him, she, too, felt the same.

" Excellent!" Tante Jeanne approved when I told her about the packed lunches. " Marie Claude is not able to come until tomorrow so now I need not worry to excess about luncheon today."

Between us, we packed up rolls and butter, cheese, ham, tomatoes and slices of Thérèse's delicious tartine. With thermoses of tea and coffee, the bags were attached securely to Ruddigore; Major and Mrs. Brigginshaw were hoisted up on to Pinafore and Patience and the two boys and Amelia went with them to bring the donkeys up again.

" It will be better if they come back until you need

them," Robert had decreed. "There isn't enough grass on our little island to give adequate herbage for long."

Françoise, he told me, was unpacking and he would be doing odd jobs around the stables for the next hour or so but after that, why didn't we all go for a swim in the river?

"Super!" I said and went off to help Tante Jeanne put the finishing touches to the bedrooms of the visitors who would be arriving tomorrow.

Lunch was an alfresco meal of cold meat, cheese and paté, spread out on the kitchen table along with several miles of bread and all of us helping ourselves when we felt hungry. Afterwards, Tante Jeanne said that she would take a quick nap but hoped that we would all enjoy our swim.

I went back to the flat and changed my jeans for a brief, towelling sun-dress over a swimsuit, collected towels and my sunglasses and met Robert coming down his steps, similarly laden.

"Not a sign of Francie," he said, looking worried, "although her car is still here."

"Well, I suppose she could be anywhere in a pretty vast area," I said consolingly.

"But not like Francie not to say where she was going."

Or whom she was going to see, I thought, but said nothing.

We found Marcel, Greg and Amelia with the faithful Perdu in the orchard and set off. At first, our way led up the same track that I had followed on the other evening but, to my relief, we took a turning to the left that soon fell sharply to the river. A jumble of mossy boulders forced it to fret and bubble between the high banks, but soon it widened into a series of deep, calm pools fringed by golden poplars and sycamores whose seed pods were already hanging in thick clusters.

Where the bank shelved steeply to form a natural diving place, then opened out immediately into a grassy hollow, Robert called a halt. It was the perfect place to swim or to lie in the sun, as the spirit moved. We all wore swim suits under our clothes and the boys stripped off immediately and plunged into the clear water but Amelia, her youthful legginess shown off to perfection in her bikini, stretched out at Robert's feet and seemed prepared to spend the rest of the afternoon there. Sufficiently removed, I hoped, to allow her to feel that she was the sole object of Robert's attention, I also lay on my back in the sunshine and stroked Perdu's silky head. I had a strong feeling that I was going to discover yet another facet of Robert Montarial's richly varied personality.

First, he questioned her about her work at school and her plans for the future. French and Art, apparently, were her best subjects.

" University, eventually, I suppose?"

Behind the big spectacles, her eyes clouded. " I don't know. It depends."

" On what, if I may ask?"

She hesitated, pulling at a root of grass as if absorbed in its tenacious properties.

" Don't tell me if you don't want to."

" No, no—it's not that. I'd like to. It's my mother, you see . . . She's an invalid. Has been ever since my father died when I was a child. Arthritis. I may . . . may have to get a job to help the family finances along."

Robert must have caught the startled jerk of my head at the stark, pathetic little statement. For a moment, our eyes met and held over Amelia's bent head. The gentle compassion in his gaze was suddenly shot through with something deeper and more personal, and I felt my own heart leap in reply. It was as if our shared sympathy for Amelia had roused an emotion quite separate from it—but just as strong.

At that precise moment, with a lark warbling high above our heads and the muted cries of the boys floating up from the river, I knew that I loved Robert Montarial; loved him not only for his gentleness and compassion but because he made my heart sing with the lark and the blood surge strongly through my veins. His eyes darkened as they looked into mine and, for the first time I think, he realised that I was no longer the unawakened young girl he had taken me to be.

I heard him say, a note of astonishment in his voice, " I had no idea!" and knew, as certainly as if we had been alone together that the words were spoken as much to me as to Amelia. But whether they were intended to show surprise at his own reactions, or recognition of my own wayward feelings, I had no way of telling. I lowered my gaze and, like Amelia, gave the blades of grass beneath my fingers the closest scrutiny.

As if in a dream, I listened to Amelia explaining how helpful neighbours and a combination of the voluntary and social services had enabled her to study for her ' O ' levels; but that it was tacitly understood by everyone that, her examinations once over, she would soon acquire a job and contribute a much-needed income to the household.

It was easy to understand how the sudden release from this atmosphere of dutiful dedication, where her own desires must have been constantly subordinated to the needs of her mother, had caused her to become a whirlwind of activity, organising her bewildered aunt and uncle into a state of near exhaustion.

Sternly quelling the undisciplined racing of my heart, I concentrated hard upon Amelia and her problems. As, clearly, Robert was also doing.

"What does your headmistress want you to do?"

"Stay on for 'A's. She seems to think," Amelia, blinking owlishly, suddenly sounded endearingly modest, "that I might get good grades."

"If your other subjects are anything like your French," said Robert, "she's quite right."

"I love the French language," said Amelia, as simply and reverently as most of her contemporaries would have admitted to a passion for a current pop star. "I think it's the most beautiful language in the world."

"I must say, I agree with you. But I could be biased, of course. And what would you like to do with your talent? Teach?"

"Not quite sure, really. I'm not too bad at art, either, you see. If there was some way," Amelia was obviously getting down to the grass roots now, in more ways than one, "that I could combine the two, it would be super."

"M.m.m." Robert seemed lost in thought for a moment. "Well, don't give up working or hoping, Amelie. If you want something enough, you get it in the end."

For my sake, as well as Amelia's, I hoped he was right.

"Thank you very much for listening, M'sieur le Duc," said Amelia matter-of-factly and with a complete lack of pretension.

"I think," he said gently, "that for such a Francophile as yourself, it would be quite in order to have a French relative or two. How about Oncle Robert?"

"Oh, *may* I? That would be wonderful!"

"And now what about joining the boys for a swim?"

"Of course! You'll come too, won't you? And Miss Purvis."

"Sally?" I suggested. And then, swiftly, in case Robert should think I was putting myself into a younger age group than his, "In England, Aunt Sallys always remind people of fun fairs and skittle alleys!"

They both laughed and then we were all, Perdu included, diving into the deliciously cool water and Robert was explaining how, many years before, his father had tied a rope from the overhanging branch of a big sycamore so that one could swing out over the water. "We'd take it in turns to see who could swing furthest before letting go!"

"Oh, let's do that again," Amelia pleaded. "It would be such fun."

"I'll look for some rope," Robert promised, "and we'll bring it tomorrow."

After ten minutes or so, I decided I needed the sun again and made for the bank. Robert and Amelia came too. Amelia pulled off her cap and her long, dark hair, glinting copper in the sunlight, swung free. Automatically, she reached for her spectacles and began to pull back her hair into its customary, severe bunches. But Robert put out a quiet hand and gently removed both bunches and spectacles.

" You don't need to wear your spectacles all the time, do you? You seemed to manage quite well without them in the pool."

" The optician did say I could start to leave them off, now and again," she admitted.

" No time like the present, then," said Robert.

" And your hair looks so pretty hanging loose." I made my small contribution to the New Look Miss Harrington.

When Greg and Marcel came clambering out a second or two later, it was soon apparent that the transformation was taking immediate effect. Greg, in fact, sat at her feet and actually used them to demonstrate to Marcel the ' old English custom ' of ' this little piggy went to market, this little piggy stayed at home!' to the accompaniment of much giggling from Amelia but no real opposition.

We walked back to the château in an untidy straggle with Amelia never leaving Robert's side. I tried not to mind. On that golden, summer afternoon, it seemed churlish to harbour resentment against anyone, let alone someone as sweet and innocent as Amelia.

ELEVEN

When we reached the courtyard, it was to find Françoise's car still there.

" She can't be far away," said Robert, beginning to look worried again.

Then, as if, perhaps, they had been waiting for us, she and Yves walked out from under the stable archway and came towards us.

" Oh, no!" I spoke almost without realising it, as I saw the expression of shocked disbelief on Robert's face. And yet, much as I dreaded the inevitable clash of wills, I knew that Françoise could do nothing else. Just as she would refuse to give up her lover, so would she also find it impossible to meet him in an atmosphere of subterfuge and deception. She must, I thought, be very like that grandfather Robert had mentioned who, given his way, would have met the Germans single-handed and on open ground.

" Go and join the boys, Amelie, will you?" Robert spoke quietly to the girl at his side, at the same time that his hand encircled my arm. I felt a flicker of gratitude that I, at least, was being allowed to stay. It was short lived. Seconds later, I was wishing I was with Amelia. Almost absent-mindedly. I had smiled a brief greeting to Yves Duprés but he, the courteous Frenchman bowed and said,

"Good afternoon, Mademoiselle Purvis!"

It was only Robert's immediate stare of astonishment that made me realise how innocently I had revealed to him that Yves and I had met since our encounter at the Country Club.

But there were other, more urgent, matters to be settled first.

"Where have you been, Françoise?" asked the head of the house of Montarial.

Her chin lifted. "Visiting Yves."

"Without my knowledge!"

"I am of age, Robert, an independent, working woman who is entitled to make her own friends."

"But not, I think, to invite them to our home without my consent."

"The visit is not of my planning, I can assure you, Montarial." Yves could keep silent no longer.

"It was my suggestion, Robert, because I could not bear to deceive you. And because I wanted to give you one final opportunity to forget the past. Robert," it was a cry from the heart, "it is not right that something that happened so long ago should be allowed to influence the happiness of other people."

Robert seemed suddenly to remember that I was not, after all, a member of the family. "It would be better, Françoise, to postpone this discussion until our tempers have cooled and we are on our own. In the meantime . . ."

I lost the remainder of his sentence as I walked away under the stable arch, hoping to reach the steps up to my flat before Robert was in the yard. But I wasn't quick enough.

" Sally!"

" Yes?" I turned back.

" I should be obliged if you would refrain, in future, from acting as go-between for my sister and Yves Duprés!" His voice was icy.

So *that* was what he thought! " As if I would do such a thing! If you think that of me you could think anything!" I was almost spluttering with indignation. " But what if it were true? Why can't your sister make her own friends without your approval?"

" You know nothing at all about it!"

" Nor do I wish to! But there is one thing I *do* know. That I should leave the château as soon as possible!"

There was an instant of shocked silence. Then, " For Tante's sake," said Robert frigidly, " I should be grateful if you would stay. For the time being, at any rate."

" I'll think about it," I said as I turned and stumped up the steps to the haven of my own door, which I slammed behind me.

I was alone with my fury. And my misery. For, whatever he might think of me, and however angrily I might speak to him, I knew that I still cared deeply for Robert Montarial.

TWELVE

That evening, visitors and residents ate together in the Great Hall. All, that is, except Françoise. Although Tante Jeanne said nothing, I guessed that she knew Françoise would be with Yves. Marcel, when he enquired as to his aunt's whereabouts, was simply told that she was ' dining out '.

As this was to be the final meal she would cook before handing over to Marie Claude, Tante Jeanne had surpassed herself by producing a superb ' coq au vin ' and Robert had brought up several bottles of wine from the cellars. Amelia, spectacles off, hair loose and wearing a smock of cream cheesecloth over a long, blue skirt, sat between her real aunt and uncle and opposite her new Uncle Robert. Obviously refreshed from their time alone on the island, the Brigginshaws could hardly take their eyes off her.

I sat between the boys at the other end of the table, and was grateful that no speech was called for between Robert and myself.

After dinner, which I insisted upon helping Thérèse to clear away, the boys and Amelia played Scrabble—' Edition Française '—with Tante Jeanne in the Garden Salon, and Robert took the Brigginshaws into the little sitting room; ostensibly to discuss the fishing in which the

Major had expressed an interest, but mainly, I suspected, to find out more about Amelia's educational prospects.

I left Thérèse to stack the dishwasher while I made coffee. After that, I would excuse myself and go to bed. Four was the right number for Scrabble and Robert wouldn't be likely to miss me.

"Sleep well, dear," said Tante Jeanne when I said goodnight.

"What time do you expect the Trasks tomorrow?" I asked.

"Some time before lunch. And the Davenports and Miss Herbert in the afternoon. There will be no need for you to get up early."

I thanked her and continued with my tray to the sitting-room. Robert and the Major were in the middle of what sounded like a lively discussion on the comparative merits of English and French universities.

"Goodnight!" I said quietly, as I put down the coffee.

"Sally, wait!" said Robert quickly. "I am coming over to the stables in a few minutes. I will walk with you."

That was the last thing I wanted! "Please don't bother! I know the way by now!" And if he considered that an impertinence, I was past caring!

Getting into bed took me no time; but getting to sleep was quite a different matter. I tossed and turned, now thinking of Françoise and Yves, now of Amelia and her invalid mother and, when I could no longer suppress them, my own feelings for Robert.

After half an hour or so, I put out my hand and

switched on my bedside lamp. Reading would be preferable to my mental meanderings.

I had been reading for about five minutes when there came a patter of sound outside my window. Surely it wasn't raining. The night had been fine and warm when I'd crossed from the chateau, with a moon swinging above the trees.

It stopped as suddenly as it had begun and I went back to my book. But then it came again, and this time I recognised it for what it was. Someone was throwing up handfuls of tiny stones against my window!

Greg must have mislaid his key. Tante Jeanne had insisted that both of us should have a latchkey to our bijou apartment and he must have left his in his room and now required Big Sister to let him in. I threw back the bed clothes and padded to the window.

" Really, Gregory!" I began as I flung it open; and found myself, for the second time that day, staring down into Robert Montarial's upturned face.

" Sally could you come down for a minute? I want to talk to you."

There was a moment of silence broken by the sudden, exquisite trill of a nightingale in the orchard.

" Please!" said le Duc de Montarial humbly.

Seconds later. I had pulled on trousers and a sweater and was running down the stone stairway.

" Come and listen to our nightingales," said Robert, tucking his hand through my arm and leading me towards the orchard fence.

But when we reached it, he turned and looked down at me. As elusive as thistledown, the scent of honeysuckle teased my nostrils.

" Sally, I want to apologise for my ridiculous accusations earlier this evening. I can only plead extreme shock at my sister's action. But I should have known that you would be as incapable of deception as she of asking for it. She told me later that you had nothing to do with her meeting with Duprés."

" I took the wrong path when I visited the farm, and found my way blocked by Ker Jean," I explained. "Yves saw me and was kind enough to let me take a short cut through his garden. He seemed a very nice person," I added hopefully.

I saw Robert's face harden in the moonlight and knew that nothing had altered between Françoise and himself. But I had no intention of provoking a further argument and, as Robert had rightly pointed out, it was nothing to do with me.

I put out my hand to him. And an ecstasy of night-ingales distilled a heady sweetness into the still air as he drew me slowly into the shelter of his arms. And kissed me. Not, as before, gently as if I were still a child but with the passionate certainty that he now held a woman in his arms. Impossible to tell if it was the night-ingales or my own heart that sang in exultation.

I felt a shiver pass through his body and his lips left mine. But his face was still close enough for me to see the moonlight in his eyes as he began to trace the curve of my cheek with a gentle finger. " Oh, Sally! I've longed to do that all day."

" Have you, Robert?"

" There's no one else, my love? No reason why I shouldn't hold you like this and—kiss you like this?" He gave a practical demonstration that left me with just enough breath to answer.

" No reason and no one."

" Good!" He bent his head once more. But then he lifted it sharply. " What's that?"

I could hear it, too. The sound of heavy breathing clearly audible on the still air.

" Sylphide?" Anxiously, he turned his head towards the door of her loose box.

I shook my head. " Not Sylphide! Just Greg—jogging home to bed!"

Sure enough, the sturdy, compact figure had trotted into the yard and skidded to an abrupt halt when he saw us.

" Thought you were having an early night!" he accused me.

" Who could sleep through that?" asked Robert, as the nightingales obligingly trilled again.

" Super backing!" agreed Greg, as if it had been his favourite pop group.

" As you say, super backing!" said Robert dryly. Briefly, he raised my hand to his lips then gave it back to me, bade us both goodnight and walked across to his own steps.

Wondering if Greg could sense my tumultuous happiness, I wished him goodnight in as normal a voice as possible and went back to my bed. Where, perversely, since I had wanted to stay awake and think about the happenings of the last few minutes, I fell instantly into a deep and untroubled sleep.

THIRTEEN

The Trasks came much earlier than we had expected. Tante Jeanne was closeted in the kitchen with Marie Claude, Robert was up at the home farm—the brief glances we had exchanged across the breakfast table had reassured me that last night was not a dream—and Amelia and the boys were saddling the donkeys for what seemed to have become the Brigginshaw's daily excursion to Les Roches. Wishing that I was wearing something rather smarter than my working jeans, I went down the front steps to meet them.

"Madame Montarial?" The slim, grey haired lady in the perfectly fitting fawn pants and brightly checked shirt, sounded doubtful.

"Duke not at home?" Her husband, a bald-headed man with kind, humorous eyes set into a skin like brown leather, stared hopefully over my shoulder. In fact, he pronounced it 'dook'. Contrary to all the findings of our game, the Trasks were American!

"Madame Montarial asked me to say that she would be with you in a moment," I said smoothly, hoping I was giving an impression of the mistress of the château adding the final touches to her already elegant toilette; and not, as I happened to know, hastily rubbing the flour off her nose in the kitchen. "And

Monsieur le Duc is up at the home farm. I'm Sally Purvis, by the way. From London, England," I added as an afterthought.

"Tod and Myra Trask, from Colorado, U.S.A." Mrs. Trask's bright brown eyes swept over the château as if assessing the chances of removing it, stone by ancient stone, to the Colorado Desert and came back to her husband. "Sure looks all we expected, honey. Towers and all!"

"Sure does!" After several seconds of reverent contemplation, Tod Trask turned his attention to the cases in the back of the big, American car. "Someone to carry the bags?" he suggested.

I pondered. Lysette and Chloe, the two little maids who had bicycled into the courtyard that morning, could be anywhere in the château and I was sure Tod Trask wouldn't let me help him.

Like an answer to prayer, Marcel and Greg suddenly appeared at the far side of the courtyard. I signalled frantically and they broke into a run. After hasty introductions, I asked Marcel if he would show the Trasks to their room. "I'm not sure that Greg would know where to find it, on his own."

"Of course, Sally!" A suitcase in each hand, Greg similarly laden, behind, Marcel set off.

"What d'you know? A dook's son for a bell-boy!" marvelled Tod, as he and his wife followed them into the château.

Half an hour later, they were drinking coffee with Tante Jeanne on the terrace, with the boys and Amelia standing by to take them on a guided tour as soon as they felt like it. It was the moment, I decided, to dash back and tidy up my bedroom and Greg's. Halfway across the courtyard, Robert came through the stable archway and started walking to meet me and I wondered if my heart would always break into waltz time when I saw him unexpectedly, like this.

As I quickened my pace to meet him, a car swept into the courtyard from the direction of Les Quatre Vents. Surely not the Davenports already! But, with a screech of brakes, it drew up beside me.

" Sally, my sweet! Surprise, surprise!"

" Nigel!" With an emotion somewhere between disbelief and horror, I stared at the handsome, laughing face, that, only a few days previously, I would have given anything to see. " What are you doing here?"

" What else but visiting my girl? Sorry I missed your phone call but Di gave me your address and said you were longing to see me. So, here I am!"

The helpful Di, I had but a moment to reflect before I was crushed in a bear-like hug, had certainly surpassed herself in her role of Cupid's messenger.

" Nigel!" I protested, wretchedly aware that Robert must be getting a completely false impression of our relationship. But my protest was silenced by a kiss that was as demanding as it was repugnant. When I at last managed to release myself, Robert had disappeared. Miserably, I turned back to Nigel.

" What happened to Jennifer Carse?"

" Jennifer Carse, sweetie? That business ended ages ago, long before I met you. I thought you realised that."

" Yes," I said dully. There were two things I realised at that moment; one, that Jennifer Carse must have found another, more exciting boy friend in Grasse and two, that I must seek out Robert as soon as possible, and convince him of Nigel's complete unimportance to me.

FOURTEEN

Several hours later, I was wondering how it was possible for anyone to become quite as elusive as Robert had, that day. After welcoming the Trasks and, so Tante Jeanne informed me, solemnly assuring Tod that he would be happy to ' give him a rundown ' on the Montarial family tree whenever he wished, he had then disappeared, with Amelia and Perdu as work-mates, until lunch-time.

I, of course, was occupied with looking after Nigel. Tante Jeanne, while scrupulously polite and hospitable towards him, seemed, to my sensitive ear, at any rate, somewhat surprised by his sudden appearance. However, when I suggested he should find somewhere else to stay in the area, she wouldn't hear of it.

" If M'sieur Nigel would not object, there is a tiny room at the top of one of the towers that is empty."

' M'sieur Nigel ', I made sure, accepted the offer with gratitude. Anyway, he was giving such a brilliant impression of a lover re-united with his loved one, he could hardly have refused a loose box next to Sylphide.

" Any chance of coming out to lunch?" he asked me.

" I think, Sally," said Tante Jeanne, overhearing the

question, " that you should take the afternoon off and spend it with your friend."

" Certainly not, thank you very much," I said as firmly as I could, without sounding actually hostile.

" Well, I must admit it would be reassuring to have your support when the Davenports and Madame Herbert arrive. Tomorrow, perhaps?"

" We'll see," I said, hoping against hope that I might, by then, have been able to convince Nigel that I no longer cared about him.

But it was not something one could discuss in front of other people. And while I had my tasks, even self-appointed ones, to perform, it was impossible to get time alone with him.

Lunch, which we all ate together—except for the Brigginshaws, marooned on Les Roches, once again—was served on the patio.

" Let us eat out of doors, as long as we can," said Tante Jeanne. " I think there may be a storm on the way."

I had noticed a sort of steely glint to the sea and that the horizon seemed considerably nearer than before. Les Roches, now completely encircled by water, looked like an island perched upon a sea of glass.

" I should take the donkeys over to collect the Brigginshaws as soon as you possibly can," Robert told the boys. He had come in to lunch with Amelia and bade Nigel a brief welcome, but seated himself as far away from him, and consequently me, as possible.

The Trasks were fascinated to discover that the château had an island all to itself. " Why don't you build a ranch house over there?" Tod asked. " A sort of hide-away from civilisation."

" I think you'd find," said Robert, "that you'd only taken civilisation with you. As it is, you can be certain of complete isolation there for a few hours at a time. It's a wonderful place for children to play undisturbed."

He glanced at Françoise, where she sat quietly between Tante Jeanne and Nigel, a minute portion of salad in front of her, as if he were about to remind her of her childhood days, but then he apparently thought better of it and turned back to the Trasks, asking them about their life in Colorado.

Françoise immediately struck up an animated conversation with Nigel, principally, as far as I could hear, about the route he had taken up from the south.

After lunch, Robert and Amelia said that they were going down to the pool to throw a rope over the branch of the sycamore tree. They would then be going for a swim to try it out. Anyone who cared to join them would be most welcome.

The Trasks said that a little walk was just what they felt like. The English friends they had been staying with lived in London and they welcomed the opportunity for some exercise in the fresh air. And, if he'd no objection, they'd welcome even more, the opportunity of taking a picture of a real live ' dook ' swinging from a rope in his bathers!

" Just like Tarzan!" said Myra Trask, admiringly.

" If you're sure," said Nigel in my ear, "that you're going to be busy—although you *are* supposed to be on holiday, for heaven's sake—Françoise will run me into Saint Pierre. I need a new set of plugs for the car and she seems to think the local garage may stock

126

them!"

"Do that," I said quietly, "but I must talk to you soon, Nigel. My feelings have changed a great deal, since I saw you last."

"Mine, too, sweetie!" he said, giving me an exuberant kiss on my cheek as he got up to go, and plainly misunderstanding me completely. Conscious that Robert could hardly have missed seeing the little exchange, I pushed back my chair and wandered over to the parapet. I hardly liked to start clearing the table while some of our guests still lingered.

"Tired, Sally?" asked Tante Jeanne, at my elbow. Am I overworking you?"

"Of course not, Tante! It's a pleasure to be able to help a little."

"But hardly fair when your boy friend turns up! And has absence made his heart grow fonder, do you suppose, Sally?"

"It seems so," I said dully.

"You don't sound too happy about the situation."

"Oh, Tante, everything seems such a mess!"

Her hand came down over mine. "Don't worry, child! Things have to get worse to get better! In the meantime, why not sit quietly in the sunshine until the Davenports arrive? Thérèse will see to the dishes."

In the event. I hadn't long to wait.

"An unusual but interesting craft," announced Greg half an hour later, coming to find me, "has been sighted on the port bow. Marcel and I are just about to take the donkeys over to the island but we'll lend a hand with the luggage first."

"Nice of you! But how ' unusual ' ?"

" Come and see for yourself."

Intrigued, I got to my feet and went through to the front door. I was just in time to see a vintage motor car—dark green with immaculate brasswork winking in the sunlight—roll majestically across the courtyard. At the wheel, sat a middle-aged gentleman wearing a tweed jacket and matching deerstalker cap. Beside him was a lady in a cotton dust coat and a large straw hat held on by a long length of gauze-like material.

Like a captain guiding his vessel into harbour, the driver gradually slackened speed and turned his car to come gently to rest beside the Trasks' enormous vehicle.

" Mon Dieu !" Tante Jeanne breathed reverently in my ear. " Quelle majesté !"

What majesty, indeed ! But more was to come. Marcel, his face alight with interest, had appeared as if by magic and was assisting the lady to the ground—a distance of at least two feet. She stood for a moment, scanning the château, saw us on the steps and started to move towards us, removing her hat as she came and winding in her scarf as if it was so much fishing line.

" After this," I said faintly, " it will come as no surprise if Rowena Herbert arrives on a horse !"

But Tante was no longer listening. She had, in fact, grown curiously still beside me, her eyes fixed on Mrs. Davenport. That lady was now revealed as a superb example of English-rose type beauty, full-blown but exquisite; a pink and white complexion combined with ash-blonde hair that could well have been the result of nature but was more likely to be that of an expensive coiffeur.

" Jeanne, cherie ! Comment ça va ? The rich,

throaty voice was unmistakably French!

"Hortense!" Tante Jeanne was running down the steps like a two year old and the next moment the two were united in a flurry of hugs and kisses that left me breathless to watch, Mr. Davenport standing by, the while, with a benevolent smile upon his face.

"Jeanne," said Hortense, releasing herself at last, "I would like you to meet Edward, my new, English husband."

"Enchantée, m'sieur!"

He bowed low over her hand with an old-fashioned courtesy. "Hortense has told me a great deal about you."

"I can imagine! And this is another dear friend of ours from England, Miss Sally Purvis. And her brother, Gregory. Marcel, you have already met, of course, Hortense, but many years ago now."

"Ah, my little Marcel!" He was kissed rapturously —I saw Greg move hastily out of range—and examined critically. "So like Veronique!" She kissed him again and turned back to Tante Jeanne. Together, they mounted the steps while Edward directed Marcel and Greg with the luggage.

"Such a tragedy!" I heard Hortense say in her deep voice. "And a friend of the family! My cousin wrote and told me of it."

Tante Jeanne made some remark. "You mean he still lives here? How dreadful for poor Robert!"

The little procession had entered the Hall, by now.

"Just think, Sally," Tante Jeanne turned to include me in the conversation, "when last I saw Hortense, she was a widowed lady, living very quietly and respectably in Paris."

"And now," said Hortense with an engaging giggle,"
I am a married lady, still living respectably, but not so
quietly in Lancashire! Edward is 'in cotton', as
they say. I saw your advertisement in the magazine,
Jeanne. I coud not *wait* to answer it! I knew you
would have no idea that Mrs. Edward Davenport would
be your old friend Hortense Rozier!"

"You are a wicked creature, chérie!"

"And how does your Robert enjoy being a 'maître
d'hôtel'?"

"You know Robert! All new experiences are enjoyable to him. Come, let me show you to your room."

They began to mount the stairs together with Marcel
and Greg and the suitcases behind. I turned to Edward.
Was he, perhaps, feeling just a little out of things?

"And what would you like to do, Mr. Davenport,
after you have recovered a little from the journey?"

"First, I will garage my car, if I may. And then I'd
like nothing better than to take a stroll, my dear, if
that is possible. I doubt if I shall see my wife again for
several hours!"

Judging by the snatches of laughter and animated
conversation drifting down the stairs, he was right.

"Anything in particular you'd like to see?" I asked.

"Preferably something old and mechanical. But that
may be difficult to arrange at a moment's notice."

I pondered. Great Aunt Louise's wheel-chair
wouldn't keep him interested for long, and the Montarials of bygone ages hadn't gone in for mediaeval
instruments of torture. Would there be any pieces of
ancient farm machinery in one of the barns? I wished

130

Robert was there to ask.

And then I remembered Tante Jeanne mentioning the mill wheel and the cider press that worked from it.

Edward seem enraptured at the idea. First, I showed him the big barn next to the stables that was to be used as a garage and where the Crate now nested peacefully, as if there for life, then went off to check the exact situation of the water mill with Marcel. As I might have realised, the way led near the pool and he and Greg decided to come with us for a swim.

They left us at a spot slightly above the river and Mr. Davenport and I stood for a moment watching Amelia swing like a pendulum on the end of the rope, then suddenly drop like a stone into the water.

" I suppose she's all right?" Edward sounded anxious and even I wondered for a second if it was all part of the game. But the next minute she had surfaced and was making for the bank while Robert reached for the rope.

Denise, I noticed, had joined the group and was sitting with the Trasks. Both Tod and Myra had cameras slung around their necks and even as we watched, Myra focused on Robert's swinging figure.

" A pleasant little house party you seem to have collected," Edward observed. " Do any of them play bridge, I wonder?"

As we turned away from the river and took a path across a field of tall, purple artichokes, I told him about the Brigginshaws and Miss Herbert, still to arrive.

The river must be making a wide curve at this point, I thought, as we saw the red roofs of Ker Jean among the trees. And then we dropped down to the grey stone mill house, sheltered by a great hedge of yellow broom.

The actual mill wheel was an enormous but graceful structure of wood and iron and Edward waxed enthusiastic over the simple efficiency of a method by which a narrow, overhead channel of water could act upon a progression of bigger and bigger wheels so that, eventually, it could generate sufficient power to drive the cider press. I unlocked the mill for him with the key Marcel had given me and left him to examine the obviously well maintained machinery at his own pace. Then I went and sat on the bank of the mill pond, listening to the cries of the swimming party wafting downstream on the still air. The sort of stillness, I reflected, that usually came before a storm.

I watched the writhing of the weeds that seemed to flourish in the pool and wondered what would happen to us all in the next few days. Would Françoise and Yves find a peaceful way out of the impasse that faced them or would Françoise sacrifice the family background that must be woven inextricably into her life? It would be a very great love that could consider taking such a final step. And what could have happened in the past to make it even remotely necessary?

I thought of Robert and myself and the bitter twist of Fate that had caused Nigel to appear at the château at such a critical moment in our relationship. I remembered the touch of his lips on mine and felt almost faint with sudden longing.

With a presentiment that Fate might have even worse things in store, I wondered if Nigel and Françoise had met up with Yves on their trip to Saint Pierre, and what the outcome of such a threesome might be.

With a despondent sigh, I stood up, brushed the twigs from my jeans and went to find Edward. I hoped Tante Jeanne had been wrong when she'd said things had to get worse before they could get better.

FIFTEEN

Gazing around the Garden Salon that evening, just before dinner, I thought that the success of the château's first house party was assured.

Tante Jeanne was standing with the Trasks in front of an old, wall tapestry depicting some ancient scene of battle and talking with obviously keen enjoyment.

Marcel had challenged Edward Davenport to a game of chess and, watched by Greg, they sat, heads bent, at a table in front of the open window, where I could see Robert pacing the terrace with Amelia's uncle; still, presumably, discussing her chances of going on to further education.

Amelia, herself, sat on a little stool before the chaise-longue where Hortense had stretched herself out. A strong rapport had been quickly established between the young girl and the older woman and, noticing the enthusiasm with which Amelia talked and the quick, graceful movements of her sun-burned arms, I thought that the friendship would do much to develop her undoubted feminine appeal.

Miss Herbert, the last guest to arrive, sat with Mrs. Brigginshaw. She had not, after all, come on horse-back —but on foot! Carrying her heavy rucksack as lightly, so Tante Jeanne had informed me, as her forty odd years, she had swung down the hill from the woods so rapidly that Tante had been hard put to reach the front door from Hortense's bedroom before Miss Herbert herself.

She was a small, wiry lady with a neat cap of greying hair and beautiful, liquid-brown eyes behind severe, horn-rimmed spectacles. At first, I gathered, Tante Jeanne had feared extreme poverty to be the reason for her being ' au pied ' but a few, discreet enquiries had revealed that Miss Herbert was, in fact a senior Civil Servant who deliberately chose this method of getting away from a very demanding and responsible job.

She also considered it to be the best way of getting to know the people of the country. " I am of Welsh origin," she had told me, " and my grandmother spoke nothing but Welsh. It is said to be very similar to the Breton tongue and I welcome the opportunity of finding out for myself."

" You must talk to Marie-Claude when she is not quite so busy," Tante Jeanne had been listening to our conversation with great interest. " She speaks the true Breton."

Now, glancing around the salon, I decided to check if Françoise and Nigel were back yet. For some reason, I was finding their disappearance faintly disturbing.

In the hall, I found Nigel, alone. " Had a good afternoon?" I enquired politely.

" Exceptionally so!" He did, in fact, look very satisfied with himself. " Françoise is great value. Her boy friend's a lucky chap."

" You've met him, then?"

" In the village. We all went off to some bay or other for a swim. I wondered if we might spend the day with them, tomorrow? Make rather a good foursome, don't you think?"

" Oh, Nigel, no!"

" For heaven's sake, why not?" He was plainly greatly taken with the idea. And then, obviously misunderstanding my objection, added, " No need to stay together *all* the time, of course. They'd like some time on their own as much as we would, I'm sure."

I didn't bother to dissillusion him. My mind was too much taken up with Robert's reaction to this cosy expedition. Now, more than ever, would he consider I was encouraging the forbidden cause of Françoise and Yves.

SIXTEEN

As I might have known, it was quite impossible to tell from Robert's impassive reaction to the idea, just *what* he thought. But I could guess.

It came out, casually enough, after dinner. It was the first time that a 'full house' had sat down in the Great Hall and Marie Claude had surpassed herself with a meal beginning, inevitably, with mussels that the boys had prised from the rocks that morning, followed by artichokes with a delicious dressing, followed by steaks 'au poivre' and ending with savoury crêpes filled with some delicious cheese mixture.

The candles had been lit, shining down upon polished wood and delicate china to make an oasis of colour against the sombre darkness of the panelled walls. Tante Jeanne, unusually elegant in a dress of lilac tulle, laughed and joked with Hortense to the amusement of her other guests, and few people would have noticed the little frown of anxiety that clouded her gaze whenever her eyes rested upon Robert. Françoise, as on the previous evening, was 'dining out'.

" What is everyone doing tomorrow?" she asked before we all got up from the table to go through to the salon for coffee.

No one—apart from the Brigginshaws—seemed to have any idea; and even they were dissuaded from crossing to Les Roches when Robert advised against it because of a probable change in the weather.

"Sally and I will be going out for the day with Françoise and Yves Duprés," said Nigel innocently.

"Indeed?" Tante Jeanne shot me a glance, obviously surprised that I hadn't told her so myself.

I raised my eyebrows and gave a small shrug, indicating, I hoped, that the matter was out of my hands.

"Where are you going?" she asked.

"We haven't decided yet," said Nigel. "Dinan, perhaps, or the cathedral at Dol. Or there is a Folklore Festival somewhere down the coast at Saint Marie."

I had a sudden flash of inspiration. "Wouldn't anyone else like to come? Miss Herbert, what about you? All those places are too far for you to reach on foot. And the bus services aren't very good, are they, Tante?"

Surely the outing would lose much of its significance if other members of the party were included? Nigel looked slightly dismayed but offered no objection and Tante Jeanne clearly thought it an excellent idea. Before we got up from the table, not only Rowena was coming, but Hortense and Edward had decided to bring Amelia while the Brigginshaws 'pottered', as they put it, and Marcel and Greg, if the destination was Sainte Marie would be pleased to honour us with their presence.

The Trasks had already seen a similar festival on the way to Saint Pierre and opted for a quiet day at the château; especially as Robert would be there. Nothing, needless to say, would have persuaded him to join the party.

"I suppose Sainte Marie will be all right with Françoise?" I asked Nigel as we rose from the table.

"I'm sure it will. As long as you're in the party," he added to my astonishment, "I don't think she'll mind where we go. And Yves is so besotted, he wouldn't even notice!"

That remark, at least, I would agree with. But Nigel's other observation surprised me. I would like to think, naturally, that my own liking and admiration for Françoise was partially reciprocated, but hardly enough to warrant foregoing a day that could be spent exclusively in Yves' company.

As I poured the coffee Marie-Claude had made, I noticed that Edward had found his bridge four. A table had been set up in the sitting room and Robert was partnering Edward against Hortense and the Major. Tante Jeanne sat with the children and the now statutory Scrabble board and Miss Herbert, I was delighted to see—and hear—had come into her own. She sat at the far end of the salon, before a big, concert grand and played Chopin nocturnes with great delicacy and feeling. Tod and Myra Trask sat on a nearby sofa with a Montarial family snapshot album open on their laps.

Nigel was nowhere to be seen. Much as I wanted to talk to him, I wasn't sorry. Tired after an eventful and, in many ways, disturbing day, the last thing I wanted was an amorous interlude with Nigel. An early night held far more appeal.

After bidding everyone goodnight, I let myself out of the front door and started across the moonlit courtyard towards the dark hollow of the stable archway. I had almost reached it when a figure came out of the shadows towards me.

"Hello, Sally!" said Nigel. "I thought I wouldn't have long to wait. Your room?" he nodded up to the flat.

"Greg's actually. And he'll be along in a minute," I said repressively.

"All set with the Scrabble board for the next hour or so, I'd have thought. Still, you may be right. There's nothing like a warm, summer night."

As if to dispute this statement, there came an ominous rattle of thunder in the distance and the moon disappeared into a wrack of cloud. I mustered what remained of my faculties.

"Nigel, I *do* want to talk to you."

"That isn't quite what I had in mind, my sweet." He put his arms around me.

How could I ever have thought him attractive?

"Nigel!" I struggled, but quite without point. He didn't play wing threequarter in his local rugby team for nothing. His lips came down on mine, hard and demanding. And producing about as much response from me as if they'd been pieces of wet rubber. I twisted my head free. "Nigel, it's no good! I don't feel the same way about you any more. Anyway, what about Jennifer Carse?"

It was a ridiculous question; and a dangerous line to have taken. Nigel immediately got the wrong idea. "So, that's it! The little, green-eyed god! My dear Sally, Jennifer Carse never meant a thing."

His mouth found mine again with a painful pressure. I tasted the tang of my own blood in my mouth and felt an arm pinion mine to my side while his free hand fumbled with the neck of my blouse. As if to illuminate the indignity of my position, the moon came sailing out of the cloud.

Suddenly, I remembered the advice of an attractive flatmate I'd once shared with, a girl considerably more experienced than myself. ' Pretend to give in, dear. He'll be so surprised, he'll fall over backwards. Then fetch him a fourpenny one!'

I had nothing to lose. I stopped struggling and pressed my body against his. As the pressure on my arms decreased, I managed to pull one free and twine it around his neck.

Imagining as he must have done, that I was at last yielding to his advances, he relaxed and would have altered his grip; except that, by now, I had managed to wriggle completely free and was standing clear of him by at least a foot.

Clear enough, in fact, to see over his shoulder to where a tall figure was running up the steps of Robert's flat. There came the grate of a key in a lock and then the slam of the door.

The next minute, I was running as swiftly up to my own front door. Not that there was any urgency now. Nigel made no attempt to follow but simply stood there, looking after me, speechless, presumably, at this summary rejection of his advances.

But it was too late, now. Robert would have seen me, apparently returning Nigel's embrace with a passion as strong as his own. The real reason would simply never occur to him. Why should it? He had already seen Nigel greeting me like a long-lost lover.

There was only one tiny fragment of hope to which I clung like a drowning man to a straw; that the figure had belonged to Françoise and not to Robert. They were both tall, Françoise had been wearing trousers when last I'd seen her, and her hair was cut nearly as short as Robert's.

Sometime during the night, the storm broke and I lay awake for what seemed like hours, listening to the beat of the rain against the windows and Sylphide's uneasy movements below, grateful that, due to Robert's foresight, the donkeys were also under cover.

SEVENTEEN

Next morning, I looked out on a changed world. Although the rain had stopped, everything was sodden. Pools of leaf-strewn water lay in the yard and Robert's petunias were crushed and battered. A branch of the fig tree had broken, swinging loose in the wind that was coming straight off the sea, bring the boom of the waves and the incessant, ghostly cry of the gulls.

I saw Robert, swathed in oilskins, go running down his steps, Perdu at his heels, and head for the château.

Would our trip to Sainte Marie still take place, I wondered, as I pulled on a pair of jeans for my morning chores. Even as I pondered, a shaft of sunlight transformed the yard into a mirror of reflected light and an optimistic thrush in the orchard whistled a brilliant cadenza. Immediately, an unpunctual Dawn Chorus was doing its best to catch up with the new day.

Taking it as an omen, I put out a sun dress of blue and green, mottled like a peacock's wing, but also added a showerproof jacket of navy gaberdine.

As I splashed my way across the the yard, revelling in the scent of wet earth and the salty tang of the spray that must be reaching high up the cliffs this morning. I found I was half hoping for, half dreading an encounter with Robert.

In spite of having to cycle from the lodge and down what must be a very muddy track this morning, Marie Claude was ahead of me in the kitchen. Her welcome face and cheerful " Bon jour, ma'amselle!" reminded me of the first time I had heard her voice directing me to the château.

I set out the early morning tea trays with pretty, rose-bud china and made an enormous cup of coffee for Tante Jeanne, hoping to get it to her while she was still in bed. But, as usual, she walked into the kitchen just as I was about to set it on a tray.

She gave an extravagant gesture of delight. " Magnifique! Comme je t'adore, Sally!" Before her first cup of coffee of the day, Tante Jeanne was quite incapable of speaking anything but her mother-tongue! She sat at the table in the big, butcher's apron she wore every morning, wrapped her fingers around the huge cup and closed her eyes in ecstatic anticipation. After her first sip, she opened one eye and gave me a radiant smile. " Now, the day can begin!"

She turned to Marie-Claude and began to question her about storm damage and I started off with my trays, and to enquire if those preferring a Continental breakfast would like it in their rooms.

In view of the watery conditions outside, most people opted for coffee and croissants in bed. Only Amelia couldn't bear the idea. From her little room in one of the towers, we looked out at the huge waves hurling themselves against the cliffs, and sending up columns of spray so high, the patio was rapidly turning into a paddling pool for the gulls.

" It makes you realise," said Amelia, " just how unimportant you really are." I looked at the wistful little face and bent to give her a quick hug.

"Everyone is important to someone," I told her. It was strange how Amelia, the prodigy whom everyone had first thought should be taken down a peg or two, in fact badly needed her confidence building up.

And who, I wondered, as I went back to the kitchen, was I important to? This unproductive train of thought brought me, reluctantly, to the realisation that I had completely forgotten to take any tea to Nigel.

"Marie-Claude," I said as I went back into the kitchen, "would you be a dear and take up M'sieur Nigel's tea for me?"

I couldn't think of any reasonable explanation to offer for what could easily be taken as laziness on my part and she, of course, didn't ask for one. But Tante Jeanne's eyes widened at me over her second cup of coffee in unashamed curiosity. However, she said nothing.

"What about Françoise's breakfast?" I asked, helping myself to coffee, as well.

"She will prepare it for herself in the flat. And for Robert, too, perhaps."

But in that, she was wrong. He came into the kitchen about an hour later, just as I was on the point of leaving. With Amelia's assistance, I had taken up the breakfast and helped Marie Claude to fill the little, individual carrier bags with our packed lunches. Robert glanced at them where they were stacked on a side table.

"So, the trip is still on?" He sounded surprised.

"You forget, Robert, that the English are a hardy race," said Tante Jeanne, with an indulgent chuckle.

But Robert didn't laugh. Instead, he looked me full in the face with an expression of such disdain in his eyes that my heart plummeted like a stone. I knew then that the faint hope I had cherished that it might have been Françoise, and not he, on the steps the previous night, could be abandoned.

My head held high, I walked past him out of the kitchen and back to the refuge of my room.

EIGHTEEN

It had been already decided, apparently, that Nigel's car should be the chosen vehicle for our expedition. Rowena Herbert, I suggested to an extremely sulky Nigel, could fit quite easily into its big, back seat, along with Françoise and myself.

This conversation, if you could call it that, took place in the barn and for a moment I thought that Nigel would refuse but Françoise, coming in at that moment, said she thought it an excellent arrangement. Especially as Yves would know the way.

" Don't *you* know it, then?" Nigel asked pointedly. But she was not to be drawn.

The three youngsters came in and climbed up into the back seat of Edward's open car. Warmly clad in anaraks and woolly caps—and a marathon scarf wound round all three of their necks!—they obviously intended enjoying every second of the expedition.

" If it rains," Edward warned them, " you will have to get out and help me put up the hood."

" It won't!" said Tante Jeanne, who had come, with the remaining guests, to wave us off. " The storm has spent itself."

Indeed, the sky had regained its former tranquility

and there was now a delicious freshness in the air that made me envy the occupants of the open car. We set off up the track to a chorus of shrieks and a doffing of caps from the children.

It had been decided that Nigel's car should lead the way, keeping its speed to the more sedate pace of the older model. As we neared Les Quatres Vents, Yves suddenly stepped forward out of the trees and, Nigel halting the car for a brief second, slid quickly into the front passenger seat. I was uncomfortably aware of plans discreetly made behind my back.

We took the coast road and this time, with Françoise answering Rowena's many questions, I was free to study the beaches we passed. Today was Saturday and one, in particular, was crowded with holiday makers, their gay umbrellas and striped bathing tents making a kaleidoscope of colour against the golden sand. The bay was almost land-locked by the sheltering arms of two headlands and the waves had lost much of the fierceness of the open sea. Indeed, close inshore, a fleet of wind gliders, like tiny rafts with only room enough for one person to stand and hold the big, very collapsible sail, raced before the breeze. As I watched, several collapsed ignominiously into the water but those who could control them moved at a fair pace. Looking back over my shoulder, I saw Greg pointing excitedly and I guessed it wouldn't be long before he wanted to try his skill.

An hour or so later, we were cutting across the neck of a wide promontory then running down into Sainte Marie, the little village at the mouth of a river where the Folklore Festival was due to begin that afternoon. Clearly, the village was ' en fête '. Strings of flags and bunting had been hung between the acacia trees that lined the main boulevard and a bandstand erected in the centre of the square.

"This way!" said Yves, after both cars had parked. 'This way' was a narrow alleyway running down between tall, gabled houses, to the river. There, beside a cobbled quay where fishing boats were tied and nets spread to dry, we found Les Mimosas, a long, white-washed building whose roof of scalloped, golden thatch seemed to grow naturally out of the grove of mimosa trees into which it nestled. Both Rowena and I stopped in our tracks, not only to appreciate the beauty of the scene but to sniff the heavenly scent of the clustered flowers.

Obviously, Yves knew it well. He settled us with our packed lunches at wooden tables under the trees then went off to organise drinks from the bar.

I saw Françoise glance over and begin to walk towards me. With a smile, I made room for her on my bench, but it was Hortense and Edward, in fact, who joined me there, beating Françoise by a short head. I saw her shrug then turn to help Yves hand round our drinks.

"Not to beat about the bush," said Edward, "we wanted to talk to you about Amelia. We know you're not directly concerned but both Hortense and I would appreciate an objective opinion from a sensible person like yourseelf."

"It doesn't take much sense," I pointed out, "to know that Amelia is a very shy but talented youngster."

"There speaks an old woman of the world!" scoffed Hortense. "But you are right, chérie. She is a very unusual child. In fact, Edward and I would like very much to adopt her!"

"Adopt! But, her mother . . ."

"We don't mean in the accepted sense of the word, of course," Edward hastened to explain. "But, as you may know, I am in the textile business in England and I'm always on the look-out for new talent, especially on the design side. If Amelia's artistic flair is anything like her languages, I could certainly use her."

"You mean, actually employ her? Isn't she rather young for that?"

"On a student pupil basis, at first, with time off for study. But we could certainly pay her a reasonable salary."

"Where would she live?"

"Well that's something we would have to go into, of course. But she and her mother live in Cheshire. Within travelling distance of our factory, I would have thought. If there are difficulties, however, we have a certain amount of staff accommodation available and her mother could come, too."

"And Amelia and I would be able to practise our French on each other," said Hortense.

"I must say, it sounds a wonderful opportunity for her," I said.

"One can't be positive, of course," said Edward, "until we have met her mother but I've sounded out her uncle and he thoroughly approves. Apparently Amelia's mother has been very worried about her brains going to waste in some second-rate job, just to bring in much-needed money."

"Now that Sally has given her approval," said

Hortense happily, " Major Brigginshaw can tell Amelia. And, if she agrees, you and I, Edward, will go and visit her mother as soon as we get back to England."

" Of course! And now, Sally, can I get you another drink?"

" Thank you, but no," I refused Edward's invitation. " I am going to lie on my coat on the grass and eat my peach."

While we had talked, we had steadily munched our way through our packed lunches, and now all I had left was a large and succulent peach.

In fact, so soothed was I by the golden fragrance above my head that I must have fallen asleep. The next I knew, Greg was shaking me and telling me that, unless I wanted to miss the procession, I had better get a move on.

As we walked back to the square behind the others, he asked me if it would be possible for us to stop on the way home and try our skill at wind-gliding. " Marcel says he knows a place where we can hire the gliders."

" We'll talk about it later," I promised, for there was now the sound of a band approaching, " but I don't see why not."

It was a shining, brass band, the players brave in scarlet and blue uniforms, that led the procession into the square and filed on to the bandstand. There, they sat, while a fife and drum band, the players in national dress, took over. There were murmurs of appreciation from the crowd at the beauty of the costumes and Rowena Herbert, standing next to me, was obviously enraptured at the sight. She brought out a little note-book from her handbag and started scribbling busily.

The men and boys wore big, broad-rimmed black hats, black velvet jackets over white shirts and brocade waistcoats, and neat, grey trousers. The girls were all in sprigged or striped over-skirts, caught up to show white, lace-trimmed petticoats and white stockings but their head covering varied from big, floppy sun bonnets and simple kerchiefs to the intricately patterned, starched lace caps.

Those who were not playing traditional French melodies on fife or drum—and several managed to play both!—carried ancient, wooden pitchforks and wide, shallow baskets filled with ears of wheat and barley.

Their heavy, wooden clogs didn't stop them dancing —back through their own ranks or round through the spectators. I saw Greg and Marcel seized and twirled by two pretty, sunburned girls and watched Amelia swept away by a tall, moustached young man.

So engrossed was I, in watching their nimble footwork, I didn't notice the two velvet-coated gentlemen bowing in front of us, until Rowena hissed, "Come on! They want to dance with us!" The next moment I was held by expert hands and twirling I hoped, with the best of them.

When the dancing was over, we were returned politely to our places. All except Rowena. Deep in conversation, she stayed with her partner, and actually went and sat with the group when the square was filled with a mixed choir, also in national costume. Everyone, of course, sang with them, mostly traditional songs with the occasional modern ballad.

I looked around me. Yves and Françoise were hand in hand and singing most of the songs to each other.

152

Hortense was obviously enjoying herself enormously and, when not singing at the top of her voice, was busily explaining various points of interest to Edward. Rowena, I could see, was scribbling in her notebook, at the dictation of her escort. Nigel, I was relieved to discover, had acquired a pretty, young Breton girl on each arm.

" Thought he was supposed to be *your* boy friend," Greg, who must have followed the direction of my eyes, hissed in my ear.

" Not any longer!"

He gave an immediate thumbs-up sign of approval. " Good! I wouldn't fancy *him* as a brother-in-law!"

And would he, I wondered, fancy Robert Montarial? Standing there in the middle of all that happy, festive crowd, I had a sudden, almost intolerable yearning for his presence by my side. Sadly, I wondered what he was doing now and if the beautiful Denise was with him.

The choir sang their last song and gave way to a series of tableaux depicting, so Yves explained, various events in the history of the little town. To end, came a group of young acrobats and then it was all over and the bars and cafés around the square were doing a roaring trade. We all sat together to drink ice-cold lemonade and Rowena came back, looking very pleased with herself.

" Many of the Breton words are identical with the Welsh," she told me enthusiastically. " I am making a list."

" I admire your singleness of purpose," I said.

After we had all studied Rowena's little note-book, the children made their formal application, as it were, to go for a swim and a 'wind-glide' at the resort we had passed through that morning. Nearly everyone, it seemed, had brought their swimming gear. Only Hortense and Edward had not. They would look round a nearby, monastic ruin instead, Hortense decreed, and it was arranged that we should all meet up outside the Hotel de la Poste just above the beach, at around six o'clock. That should give us ample time to get back to the château for eight o'clock dinner.

I think we all enjoyed our two hours on the beach. The water was very clear and salt, with just sufficient chill to make the first immersion a delightful shock after the sun's heat. From then, it was sheer bliss to float on the gentle swell and watch Greg's attempt to imitate Marcel's skill on the wind-glider.
Amelia had elected to stay with me. " I've a rotten sense of balance, anyway. I should only look a fool."

So, when Françoise suggested we swim out to a raft anchored some way from the shore, Amelia, naturally, came too. Yet again, it seemed that attempts to get me on my own had been frustrated.

" There's Miss Herbert!" Amelia waved to the slim figure seated beside our towels and clothes. Although she had brought her swim suit, she had elected only to sunbathe in it, preferring to sit and watch the holiday-ing French play boule and volley ball on the smooth sand. Yves, I noticed, had remained with her.

" And here comes Greg! Got the hang of it at last!"

He came sailing past us on his glider, arms spread wide, like Batman, to hold the sail into the wind, his body perfectly balanced on the narrow 'deck'. Marcel followed him, with the confident air of the regular glider. Greg, over-confident perhaps, lost his balance, his sail collapsed into the water and he went in after it.

"Bad luck!" Amelia jumped in to help him.

"Sally," Françoise began urgently, "now that we're on our own . . ."

"Hello, you two!" Nigel surfaced practically beneath the raft and swung himself up beside us. Françoise raised her eyes to heaven in a comic grimace of resignation and collapsed on to her back.

Soon afterwards, we swam back to the beach and Greg organised us all in a game of cricket, played with a beach ball and a piece of driftwood. Most of the French looked on in amusement but one or two actually joined in.

It was with a considerable shock that we discovered it was a quarter to seven; we were probably already keeping Hortense and Edward waiting at the Hotel de la Poste.

NINETEEN

In fact, it was gone seven before we all, as arranged, met up outside the Hotel de la Poste.

"Why don't we dine out?" Françoise suggested to our car-load.

"Oh, I don't know," I demurred. I was beginning to feel a little tired; it had been a long day and the suggestion of a headache was hovering behind my eyes. "Won't your aunt be expecting us back?"

"I happen to know it's a cold meal tonight, so nothing will spoil. I'll telephone, of course."

Something about the tone of her voice. told me she was determined that our 'foursome', at least, should stay and dine together.

"What about you?" I asked Rowena. "Would you like to join us?"

But she, as I'd half expected, declined. "If, that is, Mr. Davenport can accommodate me in his car."

"No problem, there," Edward said breezily, when approached, "the youngsters can easily squeeze up a bit."

"Will you remember the way back?" I still felt partly responsible.

"With a genuine French woman sitting beside me, we can always ask!"

"But what if you break down?"

Now, I really had said the wrong thing! "Sally, I promise you that if my car so far forgets itself as to break down *and* I am unable to fix it myself, I shall personally treat you to the largest ice-cream we can find!"

"You're on!" I said. "And I do beg your pardon."

"So I should think!"

The enormous scarf having been stretched even further to accommodate yet another neck, Edward found an extra rug and we waved them away; for all the world as if Brighton was their next stop. A group of French holiday makers even sent up a cheer.

"Mad English!" said Françoise affectionately. "Now, let's go and eat. And, I warn you. I feel like dancing, too!"

I didn't welcome the idea of being in Nigel's arms again, even on the dance floor, but I said nothing. About dancing, at least. "Françoise," I said, as we walked up the staircase of the rather smart restaurant, she and Yves had selected, "what are you up to?"

"Up to?" she made big, innocent eyes at me. "The first floor, only, I assure you, where there is a bar and dancing."

"In England," I said crisply, "being 'up to something' means having an ulterior motive for some seemingly innocent action."

She paused, gave me a penetrating look, then seized me by the hand and almost dragged me into the powder room, which we happened to be passing. Fortunately, the place was deserted.

"Françoise what *is* this?"

" Sally, please be patient a little longer. You are quite right. I *am* 'up to something', as you say, and I regret very much that it has been necessary. But Yves is to tell you everything very shortly."

" Why Yves? And is Nigel part of the mystery?"

" Yves, because he can tell you everything first hand, as it happened. And no, Nigel knows nothing of it. I will take care of him while Yves talks to you."

" I'm sure he won't have any objection to that!"

" He is what you call a 'lady shooter', n'est-ce-pas?"

" Killer," I murmured automatically. " Unless, of course, you mean line shooter. Either would be correct, I'm afraid."

" He is not, I think, for you, Sally." She looked at me anxiously. " Please do not think me impertinent, but I cannot help noticing certain things. And comparing."

Comparing with what, or whom, I didn't enquire. I went through the motions of making myself presentable for whatever the evening had in store, and we walked out to join the others.

Now that I knew something was definitely afoot, I sat back and admired the charming manner in which Françoise invited Nigel to dance and then to sit up at the bar while Yves remained with me. There was a certain poetic justice, I thought, after his tardy treatment of me, in the way in which he was being so neatly, if courteously, 'managed' by Françoise.

Yves put down the vermouth and soda I had asked for and took the seat opposite me. " Françoise will have told you, Sally, that I have a story to tell. And your help to ask."

" *My* help?"

" First listen to my story. To tell it properly, I must begin, not at the beginning, but at the end."

" That doesn't surprise me!"

" Françoise and I are very much in love with one another."

" That doesn't exactly fill me with astonishment, either!"

He gave a tiny smile. " If only that was all there was to it! But, having established that most important factor, I would now like to go back a few years. To the time when Robert's wife, Veronique, was still alive."

Now, I was very still; listening, as it were, with all my senses.

" I do not wish to spread rumours and gossip, so I will tell you only of what I am sure. She was, as you may have heard, a very beautiful and attractive woman."

I nodded. I had no wish to dwell on Veronique's personal charms.

" I had just moved in to Ker Jean. Robert's father was alive, then, and I used to go over and play chess with him. Sometimes, I would think that for someone as attractive as Veronique, it was a quiet life. Marcel was away at school. Robert came and went on his travels. I wasn't surprised when she began to go away herself; sometimes for several weeks at a time. To see her mother in England, she said. But later, I was to wonder." He paused for a moment, staring down into his glass.

" One early morning, I was driving back to Paris after a weekend at Ker Jean. I'd been working on some plans for a client and hadn't been over to the château, but I knew that Robert was away, although flying back to see his father. He was very ill by then and Tante Jeanne had moved into the château to look after him. You can imagine my surprise when I reached Les Quatres Vents—as you know, the private road to Ker Jean comes out there—and found Veronique waiting for me with a couple of suitcases. She knew the time I always went back on a Monday morning. She was shivering with the cold.

" ' Dear Yves,' she said, ' would you give me a lift to Paris? Celeste isn't well and has asked me to stay for a few days to look after her. And my car has broken down.'

" Celeste, I knew to be a mutual friend of hers and Robert. She was a single lady, living alone near Dijon, and although it seemed a little strange that Veronique should be leaving her father-in-law at that time, I thought no more about it.

" ' Why didn't you telephone me?' I asked. ' You know I'd have come and picked you up.'

" ' I didn't want to bother you,' she said. ' And a tree has come down at the end of the avenue. You could not have reached the château, anyway.'

" I was surprised at that but she didn't seem to want to talk, only to smoke incessantly. I said nothing until we were well on to the motorway and then I asked her about the health of Robert's father.

" It was then that it all came out. She broke down completely, sobbing her heart out and I could do nothing else but drive off the motorway at the next intersection and park the car.

" Between her tears, she told me that she was leaving Robert and Saint Pierre for good. Apparently, she'd had a dreadful row with her father-in-law on the previous night—they never had got on well—and she'd decided to run away to her lover, Henri Blanquart, a close friend of Robert's. She'd left the château at first light, I gathered, with her suitcases and had been waiting for ever since. No wonder she'd been shivering!

" ' And did you say nothing to anyone ?" I asked, horrified at her story.

" ' I left a note saying that I had gone.'

" ' And did you say with whom ?'

" ' Only that it was a friend of the family. I was afraid to mention a specific name in case Robert tried to get me back.' "

Yves stopped his narrative at this point. " That is, perhaps, the most significant part of my story, Sally."

I could only nod dumbly, a faint glow of understanding beginning to pierce the fog of mystery that had surrounded this man ever since I had first seen him.

" I remember sitting in that car for several minutes," Yves continued, " trying to think what was the best thing to do. Veronique didn't say anything more. At last, I told her that we were going back. That she could not do this to Robert now, when his father had not long to live. It was terminal cancer, although the old gentleman hadn't been told, of course.

" ' Go back,' I told her, ' and ask your father-in-law's forgiveness. It is a terrible thing to quarrel with someone who is dying.'

" I think it was that, more than my other suggestion —that she should try and talk to Robert about it later—

that made her agree in the end to return with me.

"So I turned the car around, got back on the motorway but going in the other direction, this time, and set off for Saint Pierre."

He paused for a long moment, swilling the remainder of his drink around his glass before draining it at a gulp. "I did not know, of course, that coming steadily towards us from the opposite direction was a certain, heavy lorry. A lorry that was to suffer a sudden brake failure and go out of control, crossing the central reservation and crashing into my vulnerable, little sports car at over fifty miles an hour."

I let out my breath in a sharp hiss of terror—as if I had been the one sitting next to the driver of that ill-fated vehicle. And told the next few words of this tragic story, myself. "And that was when she was killed."

"Outright. That, at least, was merciful. I have no first-hand knowledge of what happened immediately afterwards. I was badly hurt myself and didn't regain consciousness for several days. But friends visited me. Apart from a short paragraph in the newspapers, the accident had little publicity. A public enquiry was the last thing that Robert wanted and it would not have brought Veronique back. But the facts, as far as he was concerned, were obvious. The impact of the collision, you see, had flung my car into the air, and back on to the north-bound carriage way—running *away* from Saint Pierre. And, as a further piece of incriminating evidence, our suitcases were found in the boot of the car. There was never any doubt that *I* was the 'friend of the family' referred to in Veronique's note."

"And you didn't explain how it really was?"

He shrugged. "How could I? Robert came home to find his father dying, and his wife already dead. To inflict the final blow of revealing that one of his closest friends had been that dead wife's lover was something I couldn't bring myself to do. And there was no point. Then! I was fond of the Montarials, of course. They were my good neighbours, after all, but I had my own life, my own friends. It wasn't the end of the world for me not to see them again, and to know that Robert considered me capable of such treacherous behaviour. Françoise, you see, was no more than a rather charming adolescent, then. We were not in love."

I could only look at him in sympathetic silence. For the first time in full possession of the facts, I now understood perfectly why Robert felt as he did about Yves, and how dreadful it must have been to have discovered that his beloved younger sister had fallen in love with the same man who, he was convinced, had seduced his own wife.

"Yves," I said impulsively, "I am so very sorry for you both. It is an impossible situation. But I still don't understand completely. Why have you told *me* this? How can I possibly help you?"

He looked me straight in the eye. "Until now, telling you my story has been painful but comparatively easy. Now comes the hardest part. To put it as simply as I can, Françoise and I wonder if you would be willing to intercede for us with Robert?"

"Me?" I stared at him in utter astonishment. "Yves, believe me, I would have no more influence with Robert than ... than Françoise has at this moment." Involuntarily, I glanced across to where she and Nigel were still engaged in conversation.

"Are you so sure, Sally? Oh, I admit he may be feeling a little vexed at the moment, because this old boy friend of yours has turned up unexpectedly. But that won't last, will it?"

He seemed as confident as Françoise that Nigel meant little to me. But then, neither of them had been a witness to the little scene in the stableyard last night—a scene that could only be construed as evidence, not only of my strong feelings but, coming as it had, only twenty-four hours after I had stood in Robert's arms, a complete lack of discrimination on my part.

"Perhaps not," I said bleakly.

"You forget that I saw you dining with Robert the other evening. I may as well confess that I saw you long before you saw me. I was with friends on the other side of the restaurant and they, believe it or not, asked me who Robert Montarial's new girl friend was. You both gave a very good performance of a couple so wrapped up in each other, they were quite oblivious of everyone else around them. And afterwards, you may remember, you took a little walk together along the terrace."

I raised my hand in an instinctive gesture of protest and, to my shame, my eyes filled with quick tears as I remembered that night. Yves put out his hand to me across the table.

"Robert may not know it yet, Sally, but I'm sure that he is in love with you."

"Even if that were true, Yves, how could that make any difference to the way he felt about you?"

"To tell a lonely, bereaved man that his best friend

164

has betrayed him is one thing. To tell him when he has the girl he loves by his side, is quite another matter."

I nodded slowly. "Yes, I can see that. And, believe me, for all our sakes, I wish it were possible. But, as things are between Robert and me at the moment, I could only do harm to your cause."

He looked at me compassionately and I guessed that the look of pain in my eyes must be telling him, better than any words, that I spoke the truth.

"I am sorry, too, Sally. For all three of us. And for Robert for not realising what he is missing!"

I managed a brief smile. "Thank you. And now, I think, you should indicate to Françoise that your story is finished and that she can come back now. She must be so hungry!"

TWENTY

I am sure, during the meal that followed, that Yves, in the telepathic way of lovers, must have communicated to Françoise that there was nothing I could do to help. But it detracted not at all from her determined efforts to keep the evening from total collapse.

A bottle of wine certainly helped and Nigel, it was clear, was blissfully unaware of any emotional undercurrents. As for myself, I kept on playing over and over in my mind, as if it were a long-playing record, the story of Robert Montarial's tragic marriage. And how hurtful he must have found my apparently fickle treatment of his feelings by appearing to accept Nigel's advances.

None of us, I think, had any real regrets when the meal was over. We trooped out into the night and made for Nigel's car, parked conveniently around the corner. This time, Françoise and Yves sat in the back and I settled in the front passenger seat as far away from Nigel as possible.

He turned the ignition key. The engine gave a moody whine, as if in protest at being so rudely awakened from its slumbers, and relapsed into silence.

And remained so. Two minutes later, Nigel had the bonnet open and he and Yves were peering into the engine by the light of a torch. Then they went through that complicated routine where one person sits with his foot hovering over the accelerator and the other calls, " Try now!" But, in neither French nor English, would the formula work. The motor still remained obstinately mute.

At last, they came back to report. " I'm pretty sure it must be the starter motor," said Nigel gloomily. " Nothing I can do about it, I'm afraid. I'm really sorry, girls."

The apology and his obvious genuine regret at our predicament made my heart soften a little. " I'm sure you did all you could," I murmured.

" The only trouble is," said Yves, glancing at his watch, " that I'm quite sure there won't be a garage willing to do a repair job at ten o'clock at night."

" No buses so late, either," Françoise mused.

" Only one thing for it, then," said Nigel. " We'll have to stay here for the night."

We were all silent for a few moments. " We'd better ring the château, then," I said at last, resigning myself to the inevitable.

" Naturally," said Françoise, " I will do that. But let us first find a a hotel and I will ring from there."

But it wasn't easy, we discovered, at the height of the holiday season to discover a hotel able to provide four single rooms at a moment's notice.

" Two doubles, I can offer you, m'sieur," said the clerk at the third hotel we tried, inspecting us beneath discreetly lowered lashes, and noticing, no doubt, our lack of luggage.

" I don't think . . ." I began.

" Sally, I think we may have to take them," Françoise interrupted. " Would you mind so much sharing a room with me for just one night?"

My answering smile must have been brilliant with relief. "Of course not!"

"All right with you, Nigel?" Yves asked.

"I suppose so," said Nigel, grudgingly.

"Good! That's settled then."

"I will go and telephone now," said Françoise. "Then, shall I see you in the bar? We will have time for a night cap, I think."

In fact, we had more than one when she eventually came back. Apparently, Major Brigginshaw had answered the phone. He and his wife had only just come in from an evening stroll, and although no one seemed to be about at the moment, he had promised to find Tante Jeanne at once and deliver our message.

"Oh, good!" I began to relax.

We all did. It was as if our shared problem had at least served to unite us for a while. Before long, Nigel and I were listening to Yves and Françoise telling us about their work in Paris and we were making our own contribution about life in England.

I was just telling Françoise that, really, she must come over and see for herself when I became aware of a tall figure looming up in front of me.

"When you have quite finished your drinks, and, of course, your conversation, I shall be pleased to drive you all home!" said le Duc de Montarial in a voice of steel.

TWENTY-ONE

I shall never forget that drive back to Saint Pierre. Halfway there, it began to rain. Blinding gusts that the
wipers had difficulty in throwing off the windscreen.

I forced myself to remember the last time I had sat
beside Robert in his car. For anything was better than
living in the present nightmare that had begun when I
had looked up to find him beside me, white with fury.

Françoise had been the first to find her tongue.
"Robert! How on earth have you managed to get here
so quickly! I only rang an hour ago."

"I happened," said Robert, icily, "to be in the
vicinity. Mr. Davenport's car really did break down—
about five miles from here. I am amazed that such a
very old car was allowed to travel on its own—but that
is another matter. Naturally, I came out to pick our
visitors up. I rang the château to explain what was
happening and was given your message. After I had
arranged for a hired car to take our guests home, I
came on here."

"How did you know which hotel?" Françoise asked.
"I hadn't mentioned the name."

"Naturally not! This is the fourth one I have tried."
There was a barely perceptible pause before he added,
"I was permitted to glance at the register in each case."

169

Which probably means, I thought miserably, that he knows we have only booked two rooms between us.

Yves had stood up abruptly. " Montarial! I trust you're not inferring . . ."

" Yves, please!" said Françoise quickly. " Robert, the car really did . . ."

" While we are here," he interrupted coldly, with a swift glance around the crowded bar, " I prefer not to discuss the matter. That, I think we can leave until later."

" I agree!" Yves was also pale with fury. " And I should be obliged, Montarial, for an appointment with you at the earliest opportunity. There are many things I have to say to you."

" And I to you! Tomorrow morning, ten thirty? I have my manager coming at nine."

" Right!" It could have been a challenge to a duel they were flinging at each other.

Like naughty children, we had then, all four, risen to our feet and left the hotel, cancelling our reservations with the mystified clerk on the way.

Hire cars! I thought, now. Why hadn't *we* thought of that? And imagine Edward breaking down! At least, I was assured of an ice-cream when I saw him! Desperately, I tried to keep my mind occupied with trivial matters, but again and again it came swinging back to the appointment Robert and Yves had made for the following morning. Obviously, Yves had decided that the time had come to tell Robert the whole story, no matter what his reactions. And I couldn't in all honesty, blame him. The humiliation I had felt tonight must be nothing compared with that of Yves and Françoise.

But how would Robert take the story? With all my heart, I wished that I had the right to be with him when he heard; to try to help him pick up the pieces of his life and make him believe that the future could still have much to offer.

TWENTY-TWO

In the morning, soon after breakfast, Nigel sought me out to tell me that he was leaving. My relief must have shown in my face. " No hard feelings, Sally?"

" Of course not! Where are you going? Back to England?"

" No. To Paris for a few days. I know some people there and it will be an opportunity to improve my French."

" But I thought the Parisians always took their holidays in August."

" Not all of them. My—er—friend works in a bookshop specialising in English publications, actually, so it's her—I mean, his—busiest time of the year with the English tourists."

" Nigel," I scolded, " you don't have to pretend with me. What's her name?"

" Colette," he said sheepishly.

" Have fun, then! And now, I'll go and see Tante Jeanne about your account."

She made no secret of her pleasure at his departure. " Good! That should help a little."

I presumed she meant with accommodation, although no more guests were expected for ten days or so.

However, she was suitably courteous when Nigel bade her goodbye, " I'm sure," she told him, " that you will find Paris far more to your taste than Saint Pierre."

As he drove away, Robert came into the courtyard, presumably in expectation of Monsieur Maroc's visit. Nigel tooted his horn and waved a hand but didn't stop. Robert sketched a somewhat half-hearted salute in return and continued walking towards the front door.

" Sally," said Tante Jeanne suddenly, " would you please ask Robert if he happens to have seen my handbag? I need it rather urgently and I cannot wait because I have left something on the stove." And she vanished immediately in the direction of the kitchen.

I could do nothing else but wait, although any communication with Robert was the last thing I wanted at the moment.

" Tante Jeanne wants to know if you've seen her . . ." I began coolly, when he was nearly at the foot of the steps.

" Was that Nigel leaving?" he interrupted.

" It was."

" For good?"

" Yes," I said, rather more cheerfully. " For good. For Paris. And for a girl called Colette!"

" And you don't mind?"

There was something about the intensity of his gaze that made me seek refuge in deliberate idiocy. " I—I think it's quite a nice name," I said, " especially when you consider its literary connections. She works in a book shop, you see." It would have been a feeble joke at the best of times but now, with that peculiar, strained look on Robert's face, it was, I suppose, quite deplorable.

He was up the steps in less than a second. "Look here, Sally!" He seized me by the shoulders and shook me roughly. "This isn't the moment for humour; especially the off-beat, British variety."

"You're quite right," I said weakly. "I'm sorry."

"Are you telling me," he continued brusquely, his eyes snapping with something suspiciously like anger, "that Nigel means nothing to you?"

"Nothing at all." And then a dreadful thought struck me. "Robert," I said urgently, "please don't think . . . I mean, I'm not the sort of person who . . . there's a good explanation for . . ."

My voice trailed away as he began to shake me again, but this time rather more urgently. "Sally, will you never stop talking? Look at me!"

I did—and immediately regretted it. There were dark hollows under his eyes as if he, too, hadn't slept a wink last night. And very soon, now, Fate would deal him yet another blow. Suddenly, I loved him so much, I thought my heart would burst with the pain and the glory of it. "Robert," I began . . .

I had no idea how my sentence would finish, so it was as well perhaps, that Major Brigginshaw chose that moment to walk out of the Great Hall and practically fall over us.

"Ah, there you are, old chap! Miss Purvis!" He gave me a quick, old-fashioned bow. "Madame Montarial was trying to tell me you were down on the beach, although I knew I'd just seen you crossing the

174

courtyard!"

And so had Tante Jeanne! I thought, refusing to meet Robert's eye.

"Wondered if this might be a good moment to have a word with Amelia about her future," the Major continued. "Now that we've got it all buttoned up, so to speak. Thought *you* should be the one to tell her, old boy, as it was your idea in the first place."

"I'm not contributing much, though, apart from offering holidays here whenever she wants one," Robert said, making an obvious effort to concentrate on the matter in hand. "But I do agree it's time we should ask if the scheme meets with her approval."

Dear Robert! I thought, who says 'ask' where the Major automatically says 'tell'! "I think," I offered, "that she went down to the beach half an hour ago with the boys."

Just then, Marcel and Greg came round the corner of the château. Alone.

"Where's Amelia?" Robert called.

"Gone down to the river," Marcel called back. "Said the sea was too rough for a swim."

"The river won't exactly be like a mill pond after the storms we've had," said Robert, looking worried. "I think we should go and find her." He glanced at his watch. "I've an appointment in a few minutes but that will have to wait."

We all followed him—along the edge of the orchards and down the track that led to the river. By the time we reached it, Robert had increased his pace so much, I was almost running and Major Brigginshaw was puffing and panting well in the rear. Only the boys were keeping up.

The way that the three of them came to an abrupt halt on the bank, their heads turning quickly up-river, then down, told me that Amelia wasn't there.

But her clothes were; a tee shirt and jeans, neatly folded on the bank above the swirling currents. A bank, I suddenly realised, that was now only a matter of inches above water that, two days previously, had been a good three feet below.

"Look!" It was Greg who spoke, pointing upwards to where the rope was tied to the bough of the big sycamore tree. *Had* been tied! Now, only a jagged stump jutted out from the main trunk. The weight of something—or some one?—had clearly been too much for the branch to bear.

"Where is she?" Breathing heavily, the Major had arrived beside us.

"I don't know," said Robert tersely. He pointed upwards to the severed branch. "It must have been weakened in the storm."

"My God! You don't think Amelia . . .?"

"I don't think anything at the moment, Major. Except that we should start searching down-river. It would be easy to get into difficulties in this current and she could be clinging to the bank somewhere."

Or was he really thinking, as I was, of the mill pond only a few hundred feet away, where the weeds were thick and treacherous?

Round the first bend, the path brought us beside the garden wall of Ker Jean.

"Could Yves know anything?" I wondered aloud.

"Would you check while we carry on downstream?"

176

Robert asked briefly.

Without ceremony, and using the thick stems of an ivy for foothold, I climbed over the wall. As I started across the grass towards the cobbled yard, one of the big, glass doors opened and Françoise came out.

"Sally, how nice! Have you come to escort Yves, as well?"

I shook my head. "Françoise, I haven't time for lengthy explanations. Just tell me—have you seen Amelia Harrington this morning?"

"Amelia? Heavens, no! Should I have? I haven't even seen Yves yet. I suppose I haven't missed him, somehow? He's not at the château, already?"

Again I shook my head. "Come with me, Françoise. I'll explain as we go." And then a thought struck me. "Is Yves' car here?"

"I'll go and see." Françoise shot off around the side of the house. With seconds, she was back, now looking as worried as I was feeling. "No, it's gone. But the garage looks as if there's been a flood. Water all over the floor and a great piece taken out of the mimosa tree that grows beside the door. Sally, what *is* this?"

But I was already racing back to the river bank to find Robert. As we went, I gave Françoise the bare bones of the situation, as far as I knew it.

"We've lost Amelia. Her clothes are on the river bank but the branch is broken. The branch that had the rope round it."

"Mon Dieu!"

"Yves must have found her and brought her here. Where would he have taken her, d'you suppose? Is there a doctor in Saint Pierre? Or a hospital?"

"There is a hospital kept by the nuns just the other side of the village."

"There's Robert!" We were back on the river bank by this time and I could see Robert and the boys and the portly figure of the Major at the next bend, just before the mill. I shouted and waved and they came running back along the path. "Have you found her?"

"No, but it seems more hopeful." Quickly, Françoise and I told our story.

"So she must be alive, or he would not have driven her away so quickly. Pardon, Major!" For Amelia's uncle had winced visibly at the bald statement.

"The Hospital of Our Lady?" Françoise suggested. "Don't you think that might be where they have gone, Robert?"

"We'll telephone straight away. Will it be all right for us to use Yves' phone, Fran?"

"Of course!"

As she led the way into the house, a tiny, isolated section of my mind noted Robert's tacit acceptance of Francoise's authority as far as Yves' possessions were concerned. A shared anxiety, as I had noticed before, could remove disagreements quicker than anything. For the time being, at any rate.

Françoise looked up the number of the hospital and Robert dialled it. And we all listened, with growing tension, while the number rang out. Then someone answered and Robert spoke rapidly in French. He paused for a moment, then looked round at us.

"She is checking the admissions."

For the next thirty seconds or so, Robert stared out of the window, the Major turned something over and over in his trousers pocket, Françoise paced the floor like a caged animal and Greg and Marcel stared glumly at their feet.

At last, Robert spoke into the receiver. "You are *certain*, Sister?" There was a pause while the person at the other end spoke very emphatically. "Yes. Yes, I will. Thank you, sister."

He put down the receiver and turned back to us. He spoke very quietly. "No one answering Amelia's description has been admitted this morning. She suggests," his voice dropped even lower, "that we ring the police. Major," he crossed to the little man, who had sat down abruptly on the edge of a chair, "I can't tell you how grieved I am about this."

I got up and walked over to the window. Anything was better than watching the Major's obvious distress. And, in any case, I still found it impossible to accept the situation.

"Where does this road go to?" I pointed out of the window to the track leading away from the garage.

"To Les Quatres Vents," Marcel answered me, "and then it forks, one way to the village, the other to the château."

"Let's go back to the château, then," I suggested. "They may have news there."

No one seemed to have a better idea, so Françoise found a key from somewhere, unlocked the garden door, and we all trooped back across the fields.

It was easier, approaching the château from this side, to go in by the kitchen. Some one must have seen our dejected little procession rounding the orchard wall, because, as we reached the bottom of the steps, the kitchen door was suddenly swung open.

"Don't look so sad," said Amelia, standing there in her bikini. "The doctor is with him now!"

TWENTY-THREE

I am still a little hazy as to the exact order of the events
that followed, one on top of the other, during the next
few minutes.

I remember that I sat down, hurriedly, on the bottom
step; that Françoise rushed past me and disappeared
into the kitchen, and that Amelia started walking down
the steps towards us.

According to Greg, she then asked breezily why no
one had thought to bring her clothes up from the river
bank and he and Marcel, overcome with relief at
seeing her alive, immediately turned and went back to
fetch them.

What I do remember, very clearly, was the Major
taking off his jacket and draping it carefully around
Amelia's shoulders, and Robert sitting beside me on the
steps and rocking me gently while I wept into the comforting tweedy warmth of his jacket.

"Amelie," I heard him say above my head, "do you
feel able to tell us what happened?"

But the Major intervened. "Amelia! Are you all
right?"

"Actually," there was a sudden wobble in her voice,
"I wouldn't say no to a cup of Sally's tea."

She had it, poor lamb, with lashings of sugar; and

181

she drank it sitting up in bed with a sedative from the Doctor to follow. Her story was told in quick, short sentences that yet gave us a clear picture of what had happened.

"I could see the river was flowing too fast for a proper swim. But it looked so cool. And I was feeling so hot after walking up the cliff path. I thought, if I hung on to the rope—and just let my body float in the water for a minute or two—I'd be all right. But the branch broke. Just missed my head. And the next minute, I was bobbing about like a cork. And going downstream fast. Some one shouted. But I was swept under some willows and couldn't see. I did manage to grab a handful of the branches. And hang on. And then M'sieur Yves was suddenly in the water with me. I think he was holding on to something on the bank with one hand—and reaching for me with the other.

Anyway, I sort of crawled over him to the bank and he started to pull himself back to it. But then this great piece of wood came down the river and clonked him on the head. Hard. So then it was my turn to stop *him* being swept away!"

She stopped at that point and I said quickly, "Amelia, don't bother to tell us any more now."

"S'alright! Won't take a minute!" But her voice was getting drowsy and the last, most dramatic part of her highly dramatic narrative was delivered in a rush.

"We made it up to his house. Then he passed out. Difficult. No one else there. Saw the car—keys in it. Thought I could drive it. But hit the tree. Sorry . . . about that."

And now she really was asleep. I looked across at

Robert and her uncle on the other side of the bed. "She's a very brave girl!"

"She certainly is!" said the Major.

I glanced at Robert, wondering why he hadn't added his praises. There was a very strange look on his face. "She isn't the only one that's brave, Sally. Yves, I happen to know, can't swim a stroke!"

Major Brigginshaw didn't seem to find it at all strange that I should suddenly walk round the bed, take Robert's hand in mine and say, "There's something else you should know about his courage, Robert. And I don't suppose he's in a position to tell you himself at the moment."

In the end, though, it was Françoise who told him. Coming into Amelia's room, she took one look at my face and seemed to think that it would be all right. After, of course, we had looked in on Yves, his head swathed in bandages but now sleeping peacefully in a bed that Tante Jeanne had hastily made up in a little room next to the Garden Salon.

Françoise told her story on the patio with me still firmly holding Robert's hand.

When she had finished, he gently took back his hand and walked over to the parapet, to gaze down at the waves, spending their fury against the rocks below. I doubt if he really saw them. Then he turned back to his sister, put his arms on her shoulders and looked down into her eyes.

"Thank you for telling me, Françoise. And—please try to forgive me. I've been an obstinate fool. And don't worry too much about Henri Blanquart. Since Veronique died, he's dropped out of my life almost completely.

Now, I understand why. Sometime, I'll see him again. No man could resist Veronique's charm for long, if that was the way she wanted it. But now, if you don't mind, Fran, there are things I must say to Sally."

"Of course! And I must go back to Yves." She reached up to kiss him lightly on the cheek. "Be happy, Robert!"

And then she was gone and he was coming back to me. "This is the morning for stories, Sally. Can you bear to listen to another?"

I nodded without speaking. It seemed ungrateful that all I could think of at that moment were the words, '...no man could resist Veronique's charm for long.'

I knew exactly what he was going to say, that part of him would always belong to her; that, for the rest of his life, he would only be capable of loving in a minor key. I must, I told myself fiercely, discipline myself to be grateful for that.

"When I saw Veronique for the first time, she was dangling her feet over the end of a jetty, somewhere on the West coast of Scotland. And wearing a pair of disreputable old jeans and a white jersey that had seen better days. I thought I had never seen anyone more beautiful. Or more my sort of girl. She looked as if she could walk in all weathers, sleep out under the stars, and still produce a three-course meal in as many minutes.

I was very young and researching for my first book on the remote Scottish Islands. I fell in love with her before I had even spoken to her. And she gave every indication of feeling the same way about me. So much so that she agreed to join my small research team, there

184

and then, as a sort of general factotum, and to come back to Saint Pierre with me when the survey was completed. We were married two months later.

What I didn't know at the time was that she was on the Scottish coast not, as she had told me, because she was a student doing a vacation job in a fish canning factory, but because she was holidaying with some business tycoon on his steam yacht. They'd just had a violent quarrel, apparently, and he'd sailed without her. As far as she was concerned, I must have been an answer to prayer."

I hardly dared to breathe while he brooded quietly for a moment. " Much later, I was to discover her true values; to learn that it wasn't me she loved but the thought of the title that would be mine eventually, my position, so-called and, of course, the château that had been in my family for centuries. And to have a husband who was beginning to make some small reputation for himself as a writer, was an extra bonus, I suppose. She didn't realise it would mean many months away from home collecting material for my books. Expeditions, by the way, on which she steadfastly refused to accompany me.

For a few months, I think she was happy but then winter came and with it the storms. If you are not fond of the sea, the sound of it beating its heart out against the cliffs, hour after hour, day after day, can sap the nerves."

" I suppose so," I said softly, even though I knew it would be like music in my own ears.

" She never got on with my father—he saw through her from the start, I imagine. I think, if it hadn't been for Marcel, she would have left me long before. But, at first, she was very fond of the child; perhaps, in a curious, inverted way, he gave her the security that I could not. Her own upbringing had been very unhappy. She told me once, during one of our rare periods of intimacy, that she had never been sure who her own father was.

After Marcel was born, I didn't travel for a long time and we did manage to build up a rather shaky sort of family life. But then quarrels started again. Marcel was away at school and she began to go away herself for several weeks at a time, while I was actually still at the château. Back to England to see her mother, she said, but now, of course, I wonder.

Life became a sort of Cox and Box affair, with Tante becoming more and more of a mother to Marcel, and myself making sure that I was always at the château during his holidays, or else taking him with me on my trips. He was actually away with me when Veronique was killed."

He stopped abruptly and I wondered if that was the end of the story. But there was something more that he still had to talk out of his system; the anguish felt by an imaginative and sensitive man who had made a simple but important mistake—that of marrying the wrong woman.

"I should never have married her. Almost from the beginning, we were incompatible. You can understand now, perhaps, why I was so desperately determined not to make the same mistake again. When you came to Saint Pierre, Sally, you were all that I wanted in a woman. But, because of that, you were also someone whom I could easily hurt—just as I had Veronique. And you seemed so young. So full of charm and vitality, the world was your oyster. What right had I to ask you to share my odd way of life, to care for my teenage son?"

"I think," I pointed out, gently, "that you under-rate yourself as much as you over-rated me! And—may I remind you?—the mussels of Saint Pierre are a speciality. Far superior to any oyster!"

"Darling Sally, are you sure? Enough to marry me?"

"Very, very sure, Robert!"

His lips were even sweeter than I remembered, his touch more gentle; only the throb of his heart against mine, giving him away.

"What about Denise? Will she mind?"

"I doubt it. I've never encouraged her to hope for matrimony as far as I was concerned. We've always been friends of course, just as we will continue to be, I feel sure."

I doubted, however, if she would be quite such a regular visitor as hitherto! But this, I kept to myself.

"Just one more question, Robert. Why did you cover me with your rug on the boat? Was it because I reminded you of Veronique?"

He looked utterly astonished at the question. Then shook his head vehemently. "But you are not in the least like her! Oh, I grant you, your colouring is similar; your physique, perhaps, but what is that? No, it was because you looked so young and vulnerable. With all my heart, I wanted to protect you. You see," he smiled ruefully, "in one respect, at least, I haven't changed. At heart, I am still an incurable romantic!"

What seemed like hours, but could in fact, have been only a matter of seconds, later, Robert raised his head and looked out to sea. " If we hurry, we should just make it!"

" Make what?"

" Les Roches, of course! Before the tide cuts it off for a few hours! There are many, many things I still have to say to you."

We just made it, with Perdu running ahead of us and barking at the waves. I turned and looked back at the château, pale and beautiful against the summer sky. On the patio, I could see Tante Jeanne peering down at us. She waved.

Did a ' thumbs-up ' sign have international recognition, I wondered happily? I risked it, and laughed aloud when I saw her return it.

And then Robert was rushing me across the sand, away even from Tante Jeanne's delighted gaze and I knew that my happiness was complete.